THE
HOTTEST
NIGHT
OF THE
CENTURY

Stories by
Glenda Adams

Also by Glenda Adams

GAMES OF THE STRONG, novel
DANCING ON CORAL, novel

THE HOTTEST NIGHT OF THE CENTURY

Stories by
Glenda Adams

CANE HILL PRESS

This book was first published by Angus & Robertson Publishers, Australia, 1979. Copyright©Glenda Adams 1979.

Library of Congress Catalog Number 88-063894
Copyright©Glenda Adams 1989
All rights reserved
Printed in the United States of America
First edition
ISBN 0-943433-03-7

Cover painting by Glenda Adams
Cover photograph by Barbara Siegel
Cover design by Alice Soloway

 Produced at The Print Center., Inc., 225 Varick St., New York, NY 10014, a non-profit facility for literary and arts-related publications. (212) 206-8465

For my mother

ACKNOWLEDGMENTS

"Lies" appeared in *Transatlantic Review* no. 52, and was reprinted in *Mother Jones*.

An earlier version of "A Snake Down Under" appeared in *The Village Voice*. "The Hollow Woman" appeared in *Ms*, and in the anthology *Bitches and Sad Ladies*, Harper's Magazine Press, N.Y., 1975, and Dell paperback, 1976.

The above stories were also published in *Lies and Stories*, Inwood Press, N.Y., 1976, as were "The Hottest Night of the Century" (under the title "Sea"), "The Circle," and "Wedding."

"The Music Masters" appeared in *Statements 2*, Fiction Collective, Braziller, N.Y., 1977.

In the story "Twelfth Night, or the Passion," the extract from "The Coast" by Harold Pinter is from *Poems and Prose 1949-1977*, Harold Pinter, Eyre Methuen Ltd., London, 1978, copyright H. Pinter Ltd. In the same story, the extract by Max Frisch is reprinted from *Sketchbook: 1966-71*, copyright 1974 by Max Frisch and Geoffrey Skelton, Eyre Methuen Ltd., London, 1975. Acknowledgment for the song "You're the Top" by Cole Porter to Warner Bros. Music.

Acknowledgment also to J.R. Humphreys for his encouragement.

CONTENTS

LIES

Sometimes I tell lies, and sometimes I only tell stories, but never with intent to harm. I only want to please people and make them happy.

Father.
My father was the first man in his family to sit at a desk from Monday to Friday and use his head to support his wife and child. On Sundays he sat at the head of the table and carved roast beef.

One Sunday Uncle Roger came. He was a sailor and had just got out of the navy. He said he never wanted to see another ship as long as he lived, not even a rowing boat on a pond. He said he wanted a steady job in an office, like my father's, where he sat at a desk from nine to five. He wanted to meet girls after work and take them to the movies. He wanted to sleep safe and sound in a soft bed that didn't rock. He told us all this through his Yorkshire pudding.

My father said he'd help Uncle Roger find an office job, because he was his brother, but he'd have to start at the bottom and work his way up. My father said Uncle Roger would have to learn to eat without making a noise and not talk with his mouth full. He also said that Uncle Roger could stay with us while he looked for a job, and at the same time he could learn some table manners and learn not to say ain't and jeez.

"Ettie will teach you," my father said and turned to my mother. "Won't you, Ettie?"

"Oh, Joe, when will I have the time?" my mother said and blushed. She took the plates to the kitchen.

While she was in the kitchen my father said to Uncle Roger, in a low voice, "And if it's a girl you want, to take out to the movies, et cetera, there's always Maxine next door."

"She's not a girl," I said. "She's a woman at least, and a mother."

"She's a lady," my father said, and winked at Uncle Roger. "Maxine's definitely a lady. I give you my personal assurances."

Uncle Roger shrugged. "And what would I do with a woman with a ten-year-old kid?" And then Uncle Roger and my father burst out laughing.

"Joanne is not *just* a kid," I said. "She's my best friend. And I call Maxine Auntie Maxine."

My mother came back with the rice pudding and we talked about clearing out the back room for Uncle Roger to stay in, while he looked for a job and learned manners.

Auntie Maxine.

After lunch Auntie Maxine came and sat with my mother and my father and Uncle Roger under the willow at the back of the house. It was about ninety in the shade.

Uncle Roger wore old work pants and an undershirt, and sweated. My father wore a white shirt, a gray tie, and the pants of his navy blue suit, as if he were waiting for an emergency call at the office.

My mother wore a cotton dress, rather than a housedress, since it was Sunday. Auntie Maxine wore a black sweater without sleeves and electric-blue pedal-pushers. She flopped into a chair and stretched her legs before her and complained about the heat.

My father said to her, "Tell Roger, Maxine, how he can't go about dressed in an undershirt if he wants to be a gentleman and get a good job and marry a lady and settle down."

Auntie Maxine looked at Uncle Roger's chest and his arms and his trousers and said, "Oh, I don't know. It's a hot day, and it's Sunday, day of rest, and we're sitting out back where no one can see." She leaned over and gave Uncle Roger a punch on the arm and laughed.

Uncle Roger laughed.

But my mother got up and asked who would prefer tea with milk and who without. And she went inside.

Then Auntie Maxine said, "And even gentlemen wear undershirts, and at times even less than that." She laughed again and tapped her finger on my father's knee.

Joanne.

Joanne and I stood in the sun and made shadows. Since my name was Josephine, after my father, Joseph, and hers was Joanne, and since she was only eight months younger than I, we pretended we were sisters and sometimes twins.

We stood in the sun and made our shadows move together.

"Look at Joanne and me," I called to my father. "We're twins."

"What nonsense, what a story," my father said.

"The sun's gone to your head," said Auntie Maxine. "Come into the shade."

Mother.

My mother taught Uncle Roger manners. He told her stories about sailors, and she corrected his grammar. Sometimes when I came home from school I stayed quietly in the kitchen and listened.

They sat on the back veranda next to each other on the old couch that was waiting to be thrown out. A lot of the time they were laughing, including my mother, who usually only smiled.

"This here bloke," said Uncle Roger.

"There was a man," my mother corrected.

"There was a man, he had two old ladies. The blonde hung out in Singapore and the brunette lived in Hong Kong," said Uncle Roger.

"There was a man who had two wives. One had blonde hair and resided in Singapore. The other had brown hair and resided in Hong Kong," my mother said and giggled.

When she saw me she jumped up and told me to come and tell Uncle Roger what I'd learned in school, especially grammar. "And none of your stories," she said to me. And to Uncle Roger she said, "And don't you tell her any of your stories either."

While my mother prepared dinner Uncle Roger and I sat on the couch and talked. He put his arm around me and called me his sweetheart. Once he taught me Indian wrestling.

Then one afternoon when I came home I heard Uncle Roger's loud laugh coming from Auntie Maxine's back veranda. And I found my mother alone on our back veranda stringing beans. She called me to her and made me sit beside her.

"Now I want you to tell me the truth," she said. "Has Uncle Roger ever taken liberties with you?"

I looked closely at her face to find what answer she was looking for. "What do you mean?"

"Has he ever hugged you, or come into your room, while you were in bed, or anything like that?"

And I understood what she was asking. "Oh, sure, lots of times. He's always hugging and kissing me."

She put the newspaper with the beans on the floor beside her feet and took me on her knee and hugged me and kissed me.

"He'll have to go," she said.

"But I like Uncle Roger. I don't want him to go."

My mother stopped hugging me and held me from her, at arm's length.

"I was kidding," I said. "I don't like him. And I want him to go away."

And my mother hugged me again.

Later I heard her tell my father that Uncle Roger would have to go. "He's hugging and pawing her," she said. "He's lascivious." "Who's he pawing? Maxine?" my father answered.

"Your daughter," my mother said, softly, but she was angrier than I had ever heard her.

Finally my father said, "Oh, all right, I'll tell him in the morning."

Uncle Roger.
I decided to make my mother and father both happy and get rid of Uncle Roger for them. I got out of bed and crept to Uncle Roger's room. He stayed at Auntie Maxine's for dinner and had just come in. He was sitting on his bed.

"Hi, sweetheart," he said to me.

"Hi," I said. "You know, Uncle Roger, we're going to be needing this room."

He frowned. "What do you mean?" He stopped taking off his shoes and looked at me.

"Well, I'm going to have a little baby brother in the not too distant future, and he's going to need this room."

Uncle Roger sat up straight. "What do you mean?" he said. And he put his hands on my shoulders and looked at me closely.

I shrugged. "Oh, you know how it is. It's just one of those things. It's hush-hush. My mother doesn't want anyone to know."

And the next morning when we woke up Uncle Roger had gone with his suitcase. He had left a note saying thank you for all the hospitality but he had decided to be a sailor after all.

Terence.
My father told me I was to get a little baby brother called Terence. My mother would come home with him in a few days, he said. "Aren't you glad you're getting a brother?"

"No," I said. "I already have Joanne, who's my sister."

"I warned you about telling stories," my father said. He

looked as if he might hit me, but instead he turned and walked away from me.

"And that little baby brother isn't really my brother at all," I called after him.

He turned back to me. "What do you mean?" and he stooped down so that his head was next to mine. I looked into his eyes and searched for what I meant.

"Well," I said, "he's not really my brother because he's Uncle Roger's little baby. He belongs to Uncle Roger."

Me.

At school the teacher told us to write the story of our family. Or, if we preferred, we could write about what we did last summer. I chose to write the story of my family, and this is what I wrote:

"I have a father, mother, an Uncle Roger, and an Auntie Maxine. And there is also Joanne and a baby called Terence, who are both related to me in one way or another. At first I lived with my mother and father. Joanne lived next door with her mother, Auntie Maxine. Then Uncle Roger came. And later Terence came. And everything changed. Now, I live with my father and Auntie Maxine and Joanne. And Terence lives with my mother and Uncle Roger a long way away, in Vancouver."

The teacher called me to him. He drummed his fingers on the desk.

"Now I asked for the true story of your family, biography, not a fairy tale." He bent down close to me and looked into my face. "This isn't the real story of your family, is it? You made it up, didn't you?"

I looked for a moment into his eyes, and then I answered, "Yes, I made it all up. I thought you meant us to."

He sat back in his chair and let out his breath and smiled. "I'll overlook it this once," he said, and he patted my cheek. "But next time when I say I want the truth, then you must write the truth, and no more stories like this one, all right?"

THE HOTTEST NIGHT
OF THE CENTURY

I was born within the sound of the waves, in a house on a sandstone cliff. It was the hottest night of the century.

The night I was born my father went swimming. It was the last time he ever went willingly into the water.

My father put on his bathing trunks and climbed down the cliff path to the rocks below the house and dived into the sea. He was used to swimming in the ocean, and some mornings he even swam around the headland to the next beach.

While he could not clearly remember having decided to make such a swim that night, he assumed when he found himself in the water that he was heading south around the headland. When he had swum for some time and the familiar cliff and rock shelf had not appeared on his right, he stopped swimming and took stock of his surroundings. To his great surprise he found himself far out to sea, heading away from the land toward the horizon. He was even more surprised, when he resumed swimming, that it was not back to land that he directed himself, but along the course he had begun, toward the horizon.

After he had swum for several miles, a small fishing boat spotted him and pulled him aboard, against his objections. He told the fishermen that he was not at all tired and intended to continue his swim. When they asked him where he thought he was going, he replied New Zealand, north island, and if possible Chile.

The men brought him back to the bay and handed him over to the police. He was placed under observation at the hospital for one day and then released.

After that, my father would go only to the water's edge. He refused to wear, or even own, a bathing suit, nor would he wear shorts or go without a shirt on hot summer days. Sometimes he took off his shoes and socks and rolled his trousers above his ankles and walked along the beach or around the rocks, letting the sea lap at his feet.

I never saw any part of his body except his head, his hands, and his feet.

From three sides of our house we could see the ocean.

By the end of the day the windows were always clouded with salt, in spite of the fact that I took great care to wipe them clean every morning.

The ocean spray also corroded the gutters and caused the window frames and doors to swell and stick.

The house was old and shabby, but very beautiful.

My father often stood by the window and watched the sea. Some mornings he went to the phone box at the terminus down at the bay and called his office to say he was sick. Then he would stay by the window all day watching the sea, frowning.

I, too, watched the sea, and I was able to stay very still beside the window for long periods of time.

My father never liked me to come near him, especially when he stood by the window. I had to choose a window in another room for myself. If I refused to leave him alone, he would slam out of the room and often right out of the house, leaving rattling floors and doors behind him.

On occasion, however, he became so consumed with watching that I was able to move quietly into the room and remain near him for hours without his hearing or feeling me.

People often remarked that it was most unusual for a child to be able to stay still and quiet for more than a minute or two. People said I was an unusual child, and they were always very glad to turn to my little brother.

Everyone admired him.

He had good brown skin and very beautiful brown eyes and good, strong white teeth. He laughed often and was good-natured.

My father loved him greatly. He often said that the son would do all the things the father was being prevented from doing.

My skin was pale and the veins showed through. I was obliged to wear a large sunhat and something covering my arms and legs whenever I was on the beach.

I did not care for swimming. I hated the way the waves tossed me about against my will. I preferred to sit at the water's edge on the sand, or on the rocks at the foot of the cliff.

I sat just out of reach of the waves and they had to strain to touch me. They had to keep jumping up and falling back and jumping up again.

Sometimes, on calm days, I lay in a shallow rock pool.

My little brother loved to swim. He loved to dive and splash and laugh in the water all day.

In summer we went down to the beach every day, even during heat waves. For protection from the white sun I wrapped an old cotton bedspread about my shoulders and legs. My brother played on the sand beside me, his skin and body welcoming the sunrays. Now and then he started up and dashed into the water and splashed about until he was cool.

"How long do you think the longest story is?" I asked him once.

"As long as 'The Nose,' " he said.

"Not how long a distance, but how long a time?" I said.

"One whole hour," he said. "Or perhaps even two."

"I know a story that lasts until the sun goes down," I said.

"No you don't," he said.

I only smiled.

"Do you really?" he said.

I nodded.

"Tell it to me," he said.

"You could never listen that long," I said. "It is only just after breakfast and the sun won't go down for a whole day. You are too young and can't stay still longer than a second."

"I could so," he said.

I said nothing. He got up on his knees and pulled at my bedspread.

"Please tell it to me," he begged.

"It is a most important story," I said. "How can I be sure that you will stay still and listen?"

"I promise I'll listen, I promise," he said.

I said nothing.

"Please," he said. "Cross my heart and spit my death."

I waited for him to do so.

"Since you have sworn," I said, "I shall tell you. But I must warn you. If you stop listening, even for a moment, you will suffer untold tortures and great pain, and you may die."

He lay down on the sand beside me on his stomach. He lay rigid and attentive.

And I closed my eyes and told a story that contained one sentence for every grain of salt in the sea.

I opened my eyes when my father grabbed my shoulders and shook me and slapped me many times over my head.

"You've gone and killed your little brother," he said. "Is no one safe with you?"

The shadow of my sunhat stretched out in front of me and was long enough almost to be touched by the water. The sun was on its way behind the houses on the hill behind the beach.

My brother lay on the sand beside me. His body was swollen and had changed from nut brown to deep red. His mouth had fallen open and sand was clinging to his lips and tongue. But he was not dead.

For two weeks my brother lay on his stomach in bed. The doctor came every day to treat him for sunstroke and dress the burns on his back.

When the wounds began to heal, it became clear that the sun had left behind dark brown spots and scars, all over his beautiful back.

I was kept away from his room for the first week. When they allowed me to visit him, he turned his face to the wall.

I reminded him of the warning I had given him that day on the beach.

"You must have stopped listening," I said. "Otherwise you would not be suffering this great pain."

"I never stopped listening," he said.

But when I asked him to prove it by recounting something of what I had told, he could say nothing.

After he recovered he did not care to play with me.

Even when he was much older he refused to go anywhere with me alone, and if we happened to walk down to the terminus at the same time, he would make sure there were always six feet at least between us, and he would warn me to keep my distance.

For company my brother talked to his cat.

He kept the cat away from the house as much as possible. In the winter he allowed it into the basement, but during the warmer months the cat roamed all over the headland, coming to the house once every evening to seek him out. After it had eaten, it would sit on my brother's knee to be searched for ticks, of which there were three or four every day buried in its skin.

Once the cat did not appear for four evenings in a row, and we assumed that it had wandered off. The following week, however, as I danced in the remotest corner of our yard, I found the cat lying in the undergrowth, beneath a eucalyptus. It was dead. I knelt beside it and counted seventy-two ticks hanging from its skin.

My brother brought home a new kitten, still very young and stupid. I was dancing among the hydrangea bushes and the nasturtiums when the kitten sprang out in front of my feet, and

I kicked it. The kitten went flying across the ground and fell in the long grass. I knelt beside it. A colorless substance ran from its nose and from one ear, and it breathed noisily and with difficulty. I lay in the grass and placed the kitten under my shirt, against my nipple. But it did not revive.

I took it to the edge of the cliff and threw it over.

"You are a murderer," said my brother, who had watched me throw the kitten away.

And then he suddenly started searching all over the yard, until he found the other cat under the eucalyptus.

"You murderer," he said.

As soon as he was fifteen my brother left school, against the wishes of my parents, and went off on his own. Now and then he sent a postcard to say he was all right.

My father took me on a ferry ride across the harbor and back.

We stood at the back of the green and yellow ferry. I watched the foam churned up by the propeller. The agitated water was a pale, sickly green beside the dark bottle green of the calm. I had sweets, and I dropped the wrappers into the foam and watched them sucked under.

My father stood back, several paces behind me. When I turned around, he was watching the sky rather than the water. His chin was lifted and his gaze passed over my head.

I went and stood beside him and took his hand, startling him. He shook his hand out of my grasp.

"I love ferries," I told him. "Just us and the water all around, and everything quiet and smooth."

He turned and walked inside, jerking his head for me to follow. We leaned against the wooden rail in the center of the ferry and watched the engine.

The pistons, thick with grease, slid up and down, and as I looked down into the dark of the engine, I saw that every surface seemed to be coated with the same thick, dark grease, even the catwalks and ladders that the crew used.

"I hate it in here," I said, and I screwed up my nose. "How smelly and noisy and dirty."

I watched the engineer checking the different parts of the engine and expected him to slip on the grease. The rag that he carried was black with engine dirt, and when he mopped his forehead or wiped his hands with it he merely redistributed the patterns of the oil slicks that coated him. He was filthy from head to foot. My father talked with him about the engine and work, while I held my nose.

When we got back to the quay, it was almost dark. All those on board, having taken their Sunday trip across the harbor, crowded to one side. They pressed forward and waited for the men on the wharf to set the gangplank in place.

The ferry was a small craft, and with everyone standing on one side, the deck inclined toward the wharf.

It was low tide and the deck was two or three feet below the wharf. After the engine was turned off it took a couple of minutes for the ferry to nudge its way into position.

Some of the passengers were impatient to be off, for they had connections to make with the buses or the train. Some men, their coats over their shoulders, jumped onto the wharf before the gangplank had been fixed in place, and then they turned around and leaned back toward their girls, with outstretched arms, and called to them to jump.

Then there was a shout. One man had attempted to jump, but he had stubbed his toe on the edge of the wharf as he landed. He lost his balance and fell back into the water.

Someone quickly sat on the edge of the wharf and pushed at the ferry railing with both legs to keep it from bumping against the wharf, while the passengers on board fished the man out of the water.

He stood on the deck, covered with the slime of the tide, laughing.

I could take either a tram or a ferry to school. The tram went across the bridge and stopped almost at the gate of the school. The ferry stopped at the quay beside the docks. From the docks to the school were many stairs leading up the hill to a tunnel under the approach to the bridge.

One morning in the tunnel I met an old man. He had left the fly of his trousers open.

At home I watched for my father to come. I waited for him to put on his slippers and go to his chair by the window. I sat on his knee, quickly, before he could stop me. I put my arms around his neck and told him about the old man in the tunnel.

He pushed me off his knee and jumped up and raced from the house without bothering to change his slippers. When he came back several hours later his slippers and his trouser cuffs were soaking wet and had sand all over them. He would not talk to me or even look at me.

I told my mother about the old man in the tunnel. She sat down and wrote a note to my teacher. The next day the teacher took me aside and told me that it must have been a shock but I should try to forget what I had seen.

The headmaster announced that it was against the rules for any pupil to walk through the tunnel. Although he gave no reason for the rule, the whole school seemed to know that it was because of what I had seen in the tunnel.

During class I received a note from some of the boys saying they wanted to meet me behind the observatory after school. I said I would meet them.

When school was over I went to the headmaster's office and showed him the note. He and another teacher went to the observatory and rounded up the eight boys who were waiting for me.

The boys were caned and the headmaster sent notes to their parents warning them that their sons were a danger.

My father said I should go away to the mountains for a month for a change. I begged not to be sent away. But both my parents and the doctor said it would do me good after my experience.

I stayed at a holiday home for children. Since it was winter there were only two of us at the home, a very fat girl and myself.

The woman who cared for us made the fat girl and myself take a bath together every day. She stood over us to make sure we washed ourselves thoroughly. Then she supervised our drying, saying that she didn't want us breaking out in rashes and sores through leaving any part wet while we were under her care. She also said she would allow us to get into bed with her, since it was so cold at night.

I wrote and asked to be brought home. My father wrote back and said that I had to stay the full month. Nevertheless, the following Saturday he came in the train and brought me home, against his better judgment, he said.

The building inspector paid us a visit and condemned our house. He told us that the water falling from the leaks in the gutters had split the foundations, and since the house was so old it might well collapse.

My father decided we should move to a new house, inland. He found a little house in a flat street that always smelled dusty, even in winter and when it rained. My mother liked the house. She said it could never deteriorate since it was made of cement blocks.

It was an ugly, horrible house. Its windows were large. But there was nothing to watch through them but the flat backyard and the tall gray paling fence.

The sea was twenty miles away.

Every second Saturday I rode my bicycle to the sea, and often I did not get back home until nearly midnight.

I made a point of checking my father's shoes and trouser cuffs every night, without his noticing, but only rarely did I find traces of sand or the smell of the sea.

I met a boy with a car, and I was easily able to prevail upon him to drive me to the sea every Saturday.

Once, I stayed by the sea a particularly long time, and I did not arrive home until well after midnight. I knew that my father was not asleep.

Very early the next morning—I had only been asleep for an hour or two—my father came into my room.

"What do you think you're doing," he screamed, "staying out till all hours?"

I said nothing.

"You should be thinking of your studies and your exams," he said, "not boys."

I smiled at him.

He strode over to my bed and shook me.

I only smiled.

He kept on holding my shoulders.

"You're enough to drive a man out of his mind," he said.

He moved his hands to my neck. He touched my ears and my head. Then he put his hands over his face.

"I don't know why I try to keep on living," he cried.

"So why do you?" I asked.

He drowned three weeks later.

FRIENDS

Diana and Minerva were best friends. They had competed for the top two places in their class since they began high school. That final year they were trying for double honors in their university entrance exams. Their classmates and teachers were already speculating as to which one would be dux of the school.

They studied together at every opportunity, during the morning recess and the lunch hour and between bouts on the hockey field on sports afternoon. As the year passed and the pressure of preparing for the exams mounted, they spent every weekend together studying.

For luck Diana carried a nutmeg in the pocket of her brown serge blazer. Minerva carried an olive pit wrapped in cellophane. Their secret motto was *"Odi et amo,"* and in private they addressed each other in the vocative and declined their names.

Minerva's family took it for granted that she would excel at school, even with English as her second language. They had fled Europe before the war, and after sojourns in Israel and the United Kingdom, had ended up in Sydney, where they pursued their intellectual and cultural interests with some difficulty. They made sure, however, that Minerva kept up her violin lessons, studied Hebrew, and continued to speak French at home. They lived in a small flat near the center of the city.

Diana came from a family of policemen and tram conductors. They were fourth generation. Her parents were letting her finish high school because they suspected that education was the key to everything these days and in addition Diana was not especially good looking.

At the age of twelve Diana had argued with Minerva's father, who was a religious scholar, that the "c" in proboscis, as in "I'll give you a punch on the proboscis," should be hard and not soft, if Ciceronian pronounciation were followed, and although he had proved her wrong with an English dictionary, he had laughed at her spunk.

Diana's family lived in an old wooden house on a headland that overlooked the Pacific Ocean to the east and the beautiful harbor and bridge to the west. When Minerva stayed overnight, they got up early and before beginning on *Henry IV, Part I*, the *Aeneid*, and the theorems, they rode their bicycles to the sandstone cliff and shouted *"Odi et amo"* to the sea, and then they rode to the top of the road that ran straight down the hill to the terminus at the bay and shoulted *"Odi et amo"* toward the fishing boats and the bridge. Then they ran on the spot for ten minutes to the rhythm of *The Rape of the Lock* or a Harry Hotspur speech or whatever chemical equations they were working on. They repeated the ritual every two hours — the cliff, the road at the top of the hill, and the running on the spot to take a break from their books and to let off steam.

The road down to the bay had the steepest gradient in the state. It was so steep that it had been surfaced in concrete instead of bitumen, with furrows running from side to side, like a newly planted field, so that anything trying to go up or down would have a better chance of getting a grip. The steep road was generally deserted and Minerva and Diana were able to run on the spot at the top of the hill, right in the middle of the road, with their bicycles lying beside them. Now and then a motorist unfamiliar with the area found himself on the hill before realizing it, but everyone else used an alternative route that wound in a dog's leg down to the bay.

One morning at sunrise, as they ran, chanting, the milkman interrupted them with a wolf whistle. "What've we got here?" he called. "The Andrews Sisters?"

He was a young man, not much older than Minerva and Diana, and he was giggling at the sight of them.

Minerva and Diana always tried to look as much alike as possible, and when they stayed together on weekends they wore their gym uniforms. The unattractive bulky brown shirt and the old-fashioned flared matching shorts that came almost to their knees did not seem so ghastly when they both wore them.

"You never know what you're going to bump into these days as you go about minding your own business," the milkman said and shook his head, still giggling. Then he whistled again and said to Minerva, "Hey, gorgeous, what are you doing Sat'dy night?"

Minerva and Diana had stopped running and chanting.

"Odi," Diana said.

"Odi," Minerva agreed.

The milkman shrugged and disappeared around the back of one of the houses with his basket of bottles. His horse and cart were stopped at the side of the road, twenty feet back from the edge of the hill where the girls were standing. The horse was chewing the grass that grew beside the road. Minerva and Diana picked up their bikes and walked them toward the horse and milk cart. The horse stopped chewing to watch them approach. They came up and stood right before its nose and it moved its head and front legs away from them.

"Whoosh," Diana hissed at the horse, and it shifted about even more.

They walked all around the horse and cart, with the horse's twitching ears following them. Diana beckoned to Minerva and they backed away from the cart. The horse's ears relaxed. Then, when they were some thirty feet behind it, Diana picked up a pebble that lay on the road and hurled it with all her might. The pebble landed in the gravel beside the horse. The animal let out a frightened snort and careered off, straight forward and down the hill.

It was a most spectacular flight. At first the cart appeared to be driving the horse. Sparks flew as the creature's shoes whipped against the surface of the road. Then the hoofs appeared not to be touching the road at all.

"Oh Diana," Minerva whispered, and held her friend's arm tightly.

At the bottom of the hill the road bent slightly to the right. Instead of swerving at that point to follow the road, the horse and cart crashed straight on, through a little red hedge of salvia, and fell down a drop of three feet or so into the soft earth of a front garden. The cart turned on its side. The horse was flung to the ground, then struggled back to its feet. Milk and broken milk bottles were strewn all down the hill and over the garden.

Minerva and Diana got on their bikes and rode the short distance to Diana's house. They raced up the stairs to Diana's room, locked the door, and pressed pillows against their faces.

"I didn't mean that to happen," said Diana, crying.

Minerva rocked back and forth on the bed. She gasped for breath. "There's no telling what you'll do next, Diana. You're so original."

The adjective cheered Diana up.

Diana's mother constantly lamented that her daughter went to a school whose uniform drained away what little color she had in her face and hair and eyes, even though it was the most prestigious high school in the city. The mother pinched Diana's cheeks rapidly before she set out for school in the mornings, uttering an affectionate clucking sound to cover her disappointment at her daughter's appearance. She said it was lucky that Diana had turned out to be clever.

Minerva had the kind of golden skin and bone structure that made adults say, "Watch that one. She'll be a great beauty." She did her brown serge tunic and blazer a favor just by wearing them. Diana's mother said that the climate, wherever it was that Minerva's family had come from, must have been excellent for the skin.

At school Minerva and Diana had appropriated a secluded spot, high on a grassy bank in the corner of the school grounds, overlooking to the left the other girls rollicking about on the lawn and to the right the grounds of the boys' high school next door. They retreated to the bank as often as possible and sat there practically hidden in the long grass, for the gardener rarely hauled his mower up and down the bank. They read and recited and translated and quizzed each other.

The boys played makeshift games of soccer during their lunch hour. Once they kicked the ball too high, and it sailed right over the fence and landed at the top of the bank near where the two girls sat. It was not until a dozen or so of the boys came right to the fence and shouted at them that they became aware of what had happened. Minerva immediately jumped up and went to carry the ball down to the boys at the fence. But Diana took it from her and threw it down the bank right over the boys' heads, so that they had to run backwards, away from the fence, to catch it.

"Odi," she said. "That'll teach them to bother us."

"I was only going to give it to them," said Minerva. She had been startled at having the ball snatched from her.

After that, the boys often kicked their football at the spot on the bank, and it became clear that Diana and Minerva would soon have to find another place to talk and study without interruption, for the term was drawing to a close and exams were only a few weeks off. They were getting anxious and had started staying up later at night and getting up earlier each morning.

One lunchtime the football landed right on the pages of the little red book of Catullus they were working from. They had learned every poem and could scan every line. It must have been the boys' intention to make a direct hit, because when the book fell out of Diana's hands there was a cheer from the other side of the fence.

Instead of throwing the ball back, Diana untied the leather lacing and let the stopper out of the bladder inside. Then she sat on the ball, pressing the air out of it.

"Oh Diana," Minerva said, "why on earth did you do that? They'll be furious."

When the ball was deflated, Diana held up the limp leather. The group of boys assembled below them was silent for about two seconds. Then they started shouting. They crowded forward against the waist-high chicken wire fencing, causing it to bulge forward. The boys' shouting turned into a chant and they started calling out the school war cry. They pressed forward and swung back as the wire fence rebounded. They swayed back and forth in time to their cry.

"Crocodile, turtle, didgeridoo, you better get them before they get you."

They repeated the cry over and over, their voices rising as the fence swayed forward and backward in an ever-widening arc.

Diana put her hand in her pocket and held the nutmeg. Minerva sat still.

"Oh Minerva, your olive pit, quick, hold it," said Diana.

Minerva put her hand in her pocket and brought out the cellophane with the pit and held it in her right hand.

"Crocodile, turtle, didgeridoo, you better get them before they get you."

The fence bounced back and forth.

Then suddenly the two wooden posts that anchored the section of the fence the boys were pressing against gave way completely, and some two dozen bodies spilled into the girls' yard.

They picked themselves up and looked about. One of the boys, tall and fair, stepped forward and started walking slowly toward the bank, across the narrow piece of flat ground separating the bank from the fence. The other boys stood in silence.

The boy strode up the bank and stood over Diana. He looked right into her face. He raised his hand as if he were going to hit her. She looked right back at him. But instead of striking her, he bent down and took the deflated ball from her lap. He tucked it under his arm. Then he picked up the Catullus and ripped it in half.

He looked for a moment at Minerva, who was trembling. Her knuckles showed white as she squeezed hard on her pit. The boy smiled at her. Minerva's shoulder and hand relaxed. And she smiled back.

The next day, when Minerva and Diana came out for lunch and made for the bank, they saw that the fence had been mended and that the boys were playing their soccer in another area of the grounds, far from the fence.

"You see," Diana said. "That's all it took. Now at last we can be left in peace."

But when they climbed the bank and went to sit down in their usual spot, they found a note anchored down by a stone. "Thanks to your friend, we had to stay back after school and fix the fence. But I'll forgive you," and the "you" had been underlined, "if you come with me to the match on Saturday. Leave a note with your name and phone."

Diana handed the note to Minerva, who put it in her pocket.

They settled down and continued their work. When the bell rang at the end of the lunch hour, Diana stood up and brushed the pieces of grass from her tunic. Minerva slowly stacked her books.

"You go ahead," she said. "It'd be bad form if both of us were late."

But Diana stood over her and waited until she was ready.

The next day there was another note: "Still waiting." And the following day another: "You might at least have the courtesy to acknowledge an invitation. Tomorrow is Saturday, remember."

At the end of the hour Minerva turned to Diana and said quickly, her words tumbling out, "I think I'll go with him."

Diana shrugged.

That Saturday Diana studied alone. She studied for two hours, then rode to the cliff and the hill and ran on the spot, then went back to studying. That day it seemed as if she had only to glance at a page in order to commit it to memory. She longed for the exams to begin, so that she could reproduce it all.

At dusk, she went downstairs and took out her bicycle, to make her seventh round for the day. She got on the bike and began to pedal fast, in time to "Tiger, tiger, burning bright." She rode all the way around the headland, following all the roads and footpaths. She rode to the edge of the cliff, and then to the top of the hill overlooking the bay. But instead of stopping at the top, she kept on riding, down the steepest gradient in the state, skimming over the concrete furrows. At the bottom of the hill, at forty miles an hour, she swerved to the right, and coasted to the bay, coming to a stop at the terminus, where a bus driver, who saw it all, muttered: "God stiffen the crows. These kids."

Minerva and Diana never returned to the grassy bank to study. In those last two weeks of school before the exams they were busy with last-minute question sessions with the teachers.

In the examination hall they found themselves sitting far apart, and in the weeks that followed, as they waited for the results, they went to the beach every day but tended to sit with different groups of friends.

A SNAKE DOWN UNDER

We sat in our navy blue serge tunics with white blouses. We sat without moving, our hands on our heads, our feet squarely on the floor under our desks.

The teacher read us a story: A girl got lost in the bush. She wandered all day looking for the way back home. When night fell she took refuge in a cave and fell asleep on the rocky floor. When she awoke she saw to her dismay that a snake had come while she slept and had coiled itself on her warm lap, where it now rested peacefully. The girl did not scream or move lest the snake be aroused and bite her. She stayed still without budging the whole day and the following night, until at last the snake slid away of its own accord. The girl was shocked but unharmed.

We sat on the floor of the gym in our gym uniforms: brown shirts and old-fashioned flared shorts no higher than six inches above the knee, beige ankle socks, and brown sneakers. Our mothers had embroidered our initials in gold on the shirt pocket. We sat cross-legged in rows, our backs straight, our hands resting on our knees.

The gym mistress, in ballet slippers, stood before us, her hands clasped before her, her back straight, her stomach muscles firm. She said: If ever a snake should bite you, do not panic. Take a belt or a piece of string and tie a tourniquet around the affected limb between the bite and the heart. Take a sharp knife or razor blade. Make a series of cuts, criss-cross, over the bite. Then suck at the cuts to remove the poison. Do not swallow. Spit out the blood and the poison. If you have a cut on your gum or lip, get a friend to suck out the poison instead. Then go to the nearest doctor. Try to kill the snake and take it with you. Otherwise, note carefully its distinguishing features.

My friend at school was caught with a copy of *East of Eden*. The headmistress called a special assembly. We stood in rows, at attention, eyes front, half an arm's distance from each other.

The headmistress said: One girl, and I shan't name names, has been reading a book that is highly unsuitable for high school pupils. I shan't name the book, but you know which book I mean. If I find that book inside the school gates again, I will take serious measures. It is hard for some of you to know what is right and what is wrong. Just remember this. If you are thinking of doing something, ask yourself: Could I tell my mother about this? If the answer is no, then you can be sure you are doing something wrong.

I know of a girl who went bushwalking and sat on a snake curled up on a rock in the sun. The snake bit her. But since she was with a group that included boys, she was too embarrassed to say anything. So she kept on walking, until the poison overcame her. She fell ill and only then did she admit that a snake had bitten her on a very private part. But it was too late to help her. She died.

When I was sixteen my mother encouraged me to telephone a boy and ask him to be my partner for the school dance. She said: You are old enough to decide who you want to go out with and who you don't want to go out with. I trust you completely.

After that I went out with a Roman Catholic, then an immigrant Dutchman, then an Indonesian.

My mother asked me what I thought I was doing. She said: You can go out with anyone you like as long as it's someone nice.

In the museum were two photographs. In the first, a snake had bitten and killed a young goat. In the second, the snake's jaws were stretched open and the goat was half inside the snake. The outline of the goat's body was visible within the body of the snake. The caption read: Snake trying to eat goat. Once snake begins to eat, it cannot stop. Jaws work like conveyor belt.

A girl on our street suddenly left and went to Queensland for six months. My mother said it was because she had gone too far. She said to me: You know, don't you, that if anything ever happens to you, you can come to me for help. But of course I know you won't ever have to, because you wouldn't ever do anything like that.

Forty minutes of scripture a week was compulsory in all state schools. The Church of England girls sat with hands flat on the desks to preclude fidgeting and note passing. A lay preacher stood before us, his arms upstretched to heaven, his hands and voice shaking. He said: Fornication is a sin and evil. I kissed only one woman, once, before I married. And that was the woman who became my wife. The day I asked her to marry me and she said yes, we sealed our vow with a kiss. I have looked upon no other woman.

I encountered my first snake when I went for an early morning walk beside a wheat field in France. I walked gazing at the sky. When I felt a movement on my leg I looked down. Across my instep rested the tail of a tweedy-skinned snake. The rest of its body was inside the leg of my jeans, resting against my own bare leg. The head was at my knee.

I broke the rules. I screamed and kicked and stamped. The snake fell out of my jeans in a heap and fled into the wheat. I ran back to the house crying.

My friend said, "Did it offer you an apple?"

THE CIRCLE

Although I went out with Pete quite often, I did not really register his presence, he did not really intrude, until the week we went skiing.

We stayed with a dozen fellow students in a run-down little hut in an isolated valley.

I preferred to spend my day walking about the valley and the hills on my skis, rather than going up and down a ski run. Early in the week I found an old pair of sealskins in one of the cupboards. It was easy enough to fit them on my skis, and I was then able to venture farther afield, walking straight up hills and covering more ground than I imagined I could.

In the mornings I set off alone up the hill behind the hut. It was the only hut for several miles around, and after I had climbed only a short way the gum trees and convex slope obscured the hut altogether, although I could still see across the valley, through the trees, and look down on the slope where the others spent their day floundering about.

They were all beginners. They would fall out of the hut every morning and crash down to the lake's edge, and with much shouting and thrashing about they would make their way across the dam to the other side where they had rigged up a primitive nutcracker tow.

The old iron support poles with pulley wheels had been driven into the ground some years ago, probably to aid the building of the dam. Pete and the others had lugged an old car engine to the top of the row of iron stakes. And it was this old motor that propelled the rope that hauled the skiers to the top of the slope.

As I stood at the top of the ridge far above them I could see them frolicking about, little black creatures, and sometimes I could make out the little colored threads and dots of scarves and mittens and caps. I tried to measure these little creatures as they moved about down there, but I had difficulty finding anything that was the right size.

They were smaller than the diameter of a threepenny piece. They were smaller than the smallest gumleaf I could find at that time of year, and smaller than the tab on the zipper of my parka.

One morning, before setting out, I placed a peppercorn and some other small objects from the hut in my parka pocket. When I got to the top of the hill and tried to measure the others down in the valley, I found that they matched the peppercorn exactly.

My aim was to ski around the valley. I ranged about the hills, following the ridges and hoping to find one set of ridges that would lead me around the other side. I could sometimes hear the chug of the car engine working the tow, when the wind was blowing up the valley toward me.

No one took any notice of me, or bothered me, or tried to interfere with my daily program. Except Pete.

"Hell, why do you always have to be so different?" he said one morning outside the hut.

I was strapping on the sealskins. He was fastening his nutcracker to his belt.

"Why do you have to go off on your own all the time, like Lady Muck?"

"Sh," I said, "hush." And I winced inside me, for his words were loud and jarring. I looked at the icicles hanging from the gums, expecting them to shatter. "Hush, Pete."

"Be damned," he shouted, and he threw the nutcracker at the trees. It smashed into the leaves. The icicles broke off and fell into the snow.

Pete had to propel himself on his skis over to the trees and grovel about in the snow searching for the nutcracker.

I set off quickly, walking straight up the hill. The sensation of walking against the grain of the sealskins and with the grain of the slope, instead of tacking back and forth, never failed to excite me. I felt like a fly or a lizard. And on the days when the sky was low and as white as the snow itself, I felt it would take only a small effort to continue to walk across the sky to the other side of the valley.

"Hey," Pete shouted behind me. "I'm coming with you. Wait for me."

Although I was a good thirty feet above him, I could hear his puffing and grunting as he tried to follow me. I did not stop. Nor did I look back. I did not want to carry his face with me into the day. I knew he would have to give up his attempt to follow me, since he did not have skins, and he was not adroit on skis.

That night there was a great wind. It tossed the snow and caused the ice on the gutters to fall. The ice crashed and banged against the wall of the hut.

I lay in bed and fixed my mind on the ridges and the snow and the sky. The others, in their bunks in a row beside me, seemed to sleep oblivious of the noise outside. The wind continued to batter our little hut. It forced the door open, and snow blew in and fluttered about the room before settling and melting. At almost the same instant one of the windows near my bunk was shaken loose. It fell outward and swung back and forth, held to the hut by one hinge. Pete, who was in the bunk beneath me, sprang out of bed.

Instead of running to the window to fix it shut, he stood beside me and put his hand into my sleeping bag.

"Are you all right?" he said.

I stared at him. "Fix the window," I said.

And like a chicken without a head he ran barefoot in his pajamas out the door of the hut into the snow and around to the window. He seized the hanging window frame and tried to push it into place, but it kept falling back out. Then he took off his pajama coat and used it to wedge the window in and keep it firm.

Pete came back inside and stood beside me. He was shaking. His body was mottled blue and pink and white. Except for his feet. He had cut his feet on the ice and fresh blood trickled over one instep and between his toes.

He looked a little dazed. "I don't know why I did it, but I closed your window for you," he said. "Don't I deserve a reward of some sort?"

I looked at him closely. He shook his head and put his hand to his forehead. Then he looked back to me.

"Come on," he said. "What's the matter with you? I'm coming up."

He hoisted himself onto my bunk, unzipped my sleeping bag, and snuggled in beside me. He pressed his ice-cold body against me. He placed the soles of his feet against my insteps and I could feel the vague warmth and wetness of blood coming from the cuts on his feet.

"You're so warm," he said. "I love you."

I closed my eyes and went over in my mind's eye the path I had to follow the next day.

The next morning I eased myself out of bed, trying not to awaken Pete. I wanted to get away without having to hear his words. He had fallen asleep with his arms and legs so entwined about me that I felt caught in a web.

Before putting on my skis and setting out, I walked around the hut to the window that had fallen out the night before. One of the sleeves of Pete's pajama coat flapped about in the light breeze. Beneath the window were bright patches of Pete's blood, staining the hard snow. I stamped and jumped on the stains with all my might and the red snow disintegrated. And I

50

followed the blood spots back to the door, stamping them out with each step.

Pete was waiting for me at the door of the hut. He grabbed me and tried to kiss me. He nuzzled at my neck.

"Where do you think you're going?" he said. "I'm not letting you out of my sight today. You're staying with me."

I shook myself free and quickly fastened on my skis.

"What's the matter with you?" he said. "We're lovers, aren't we? And lovers are supposed to stay together and love each other, aren't they?"

"Sh. Must you bring everything crashing down with your words?"

I set out up the hill.

"You bitch," Pete shouted after me.

I walked straight up the hill, quickly and steadily. Normally I rested a couple of times on the way up and took in the scene about me. That day I did not pause until I reached the top. I could see the others way down beneath me. I took the peppercorn out of my pocket and measured the little creatures. I thought I could tell which one was Pete, for he wore a red scarf.

When I had measured Pete sufficiently I took off my skis and lay down in the snow. I placed the peppercorn in my mouth and cracked it in two with my teeth. I chewed it into tiny grains and swallowed it.

Without hesitation I found my way to the new ridge. The snow and the air offered no resistance to my passage, but rather helped me and encouraged me and made way for me. I inhaled and exhaled with ease, never tiring, and I had no need to stop to catch my breath.

At the end of the day I was on the other side of the valley, exactly opposite the spot where I had started. There was the hut, small and black, down on the other side.

It grew dark as I made my way through the trees and rocks toward the lake at the bottom of the valley. I broke from the trees and glided down to the dam. I walked across the dam and up to the hut, completing my circle.

Pete was sitting in the middle of the room surrounded by the others. He was actually lying down, across the car seat that formed our most comfortable sitting place. The others, seated on pillows on the floor or on the lower bunks, looked up at me when I came in.

Pete held a glass with an inch of golden brandy in it. He looked at me quickly when I came in, then lowered his gaze and sipped at his glass.

"You really missed something today," they said.

I looked at them. One of the girls was sitting on the floor near Pete, holding his hand and stroking it. She got to her knees and turned down the neck of his sweater. There was a thick, dark red line around the base of Pete's neck. I knelt beside him and touched the mark. It was swollen. A dark red welt.

"He got caught in the tow," they told me. "His scarf, that is. His scarf wound round the rope of the tow without him noticing. Then when he got to the top of the tow and let go of the rope he was dragged forward by his scarf. And then it got caught in the motor and started winding around the pulley wheel. It got tighter and tighter around his neck. If someone hadn't turned the engine off in time, he would have been strangled or else had his head mashed to bits in the motor."

Pete was looking at me again. I had to close my eyes. When I opened them again everyone had gone back to talking and moving about. Pete beckoned me, and I leaned down to him.

"You can forget all about us," he said. "I've had it with you. If you don't want to be my girl and stay with me, if you want to go off and sleep by yourself and ski by yourself, that's okay with me. Why should I care?"

I stood up and went away from him.

Every day for the rest of the week I skied around the valley, retracing my circle. And I spent the remaining nights in my ice cave.

That day I found the right ridge, the one that would lead me around the valley, and I planned to get an early start the following day and at last complete my circle.

I retraced my tracks. The snow had iced over and allowed my skis to pass with a minimum of resistance, and I glided smoothly down to the hut. When I arrived it was already dark and very cold. I decided to sleep outside, in the hole we had dug for the meat and the food.

"You're crazy," said Pete. "You can't leave me alone like that. Not tonight. We're lovers."

"It's too hot in the hut," I told him.

The hole was some twenty feet from the hut. It was like a burrow. I sat down at the entrance and slid down the four rough steps cut into the snow. The steps led into a round cave, hollowed out of the drift, about seven feet in diameter. The food was stacked on ledges cut into the snow walls. There was enough room on the floor of the hole for me to make my bed. I spread a plastic groundsheet on the snow. Then I spread newspapers and magazines on the plastic. I brought out the straw mattress from my bunk and my sleeping bag. Pete followed me out.

"For goodness' sake," he said. "What are you trying to prove? I can't imagine what's bugging you. I love you. I wanted to sleep with you. I still want to sleep with you."

"Please don't shout," I begged him. I was sitting at the entrance to the hole, and I began to ease myself downwards.

"You're crazy," he shouted. "And you expect me to stay calm while you bury yourself in the snow. You'll be dead by tomorrow."

"Sh. You'll break the hole with your shouting. You'll make the hole collapse on me if you cause so many sound waves."

I ducked my head and slid forward. I was in my cave.

Pete lowered his voice. "Come out," he whispered.

I took the sheet of plywood that we used as a cover for the hole to protect the food from foxes, and I pushed it up into the opening, blotting out Pete's face.

I crawled into my sleeping bag. Although it was dark outside, with only a small moon, the inside of the hole glowed with a dull, dark blue light, as if it generated its own light and life.

I slept profoundly and strongly, absorbing the blue life of the snow hole, and I set off the next morning to walk to the other side of the valley.

That day the sky was low and white. There was no color. The trees were black and I was black against the snow and the sky. I walked up the side of the hill, slipping upwards through the air and the snow.

At the top I looked back into the valley, at the others randomly careering about their slope. I took out the peppercorn and measured them, one by one, until I located Pete. I measured Pete for some time. I was still breathing heavily from the climb, and my hand shook, so that it was difficult to hold the peppercorn still enough.

THE MUSIC MASTERS

Everybody knows that men are the true artists. Where are your great women composers, conductors? Some women think they can sing, but it's more often a screech or a scream. They can also dance a little. But where are your famous women painters, comedians? Women have no sense of humor. But they are educable.

The father sits at the kitchen table with his daughter, listening to the "Spike Jones Half Hour" on the radio. She isn't allowed to talk or clatter plates because he doesn't want her to miss a word. Chewing gum on the rail, Cabbage ahead, and Here comes Beezelbom—are among the funniest lines ever written.

This father travels the length and breadth of the city for a Marx Brothers rerun. He takes the daughter to the Prince Edward to see *A Night at the Opera* and *Duck Soup*, to supplement her regular education.

When Gummo's sweetheart sings a love song from the deck of the passenger liner taking her to New York, the father groans and holds his ears.

"God love a duck," he says. "Screeching women."

During the intermission, the spotlight falls on one of the balcony boxes, where Noreen and her Hammond organ, a special feature, are waiting. Noreen wears a strapless blue lame evening dress. Her sparkling silver hair is set in corrugated waves. Her back is as fresh and round and pink as a new velvet pincushion. She sways and bends over the organ, pressing out "Melody of Love."

Take me in your arms dear
Ten-der-ly

"Why did they have to bring her on and spoil it all?" the father says.

It's a jolly day, today's the wedding
Of the little painted doll.

"God stiffen the crows," the father hoots. He hates Noreen and her organ. The daughter thinks she is rather beautiful.

When it is time for *Duck Soup*, Noreen turns to the audience and, still sitting on her stool and playing with one hand, she bows. The lights go off and Noreen and the organ disappear.

"There ought to be a law," the father says.

His favorite scene in *Duck Soup* is at the end, when they all throw edible items at the female singer. He laughs so hard he has to push his dentures back into place.

On the way home, the father tells the daughter that the best movie ever made is *Treasure Island*, because there is only one woman in it, right at the beginning. Once you bring women into it, art is ruined. The Marx Brothers do very well, considering.

The father plays the piano. He specializes in honky-tonk and thinks Knuckles O'Toole is the greatest.

The father can play any tune in the world. The daughter can ask for anything at all and he can play it. He always plays in G major, with the left hand very low and the right hand very high, so that it is impossible to sing with him.

When he plays he beats his foot on the floor. He has worn a hole in the carpet. The daughter stands beside him, waiting for a space between the songs to ask him something. He is playing a medley and there is no space. He calls to her to speak up, because he can play and keep time with his foot and listen to her, too.

The mother likes to sing as she hangs out the clothes. Usually she sings

> *I'll be loving you, always.*
> *With a love that's true, always.*

She also likes to sing

> *Now at last the door of my dreams is swinging wide*
> *There upon the threshold stands the blushing bride.*

Often the father requests that she put clothes pegs in her mouth.

The son plays the drums. He has a rubber practice pad that he takes with him everywhere. Whenever he has a spare moment, he takes his sticks out of his back pocket and beats out a two-four, or a four-four, or a six-eight. When anyone speaks to him, he frowns and keeps on playing, his head held critically to one side. People give up trying to talk to him.

The daughter thinks that perhaps she will be a dancer. She has seen every ballet movie.

She has seen *Tales of Hoffmann*. Olympia, the wooden doll, is so lifelike that a young student falls in love with her. But she is only a piece of wood, a puppet.

She has seen *The Red Shoes*. When the girl accepts the red shoes and puts them on, she dances forever. The shoes don't let her rest and they dance her to death.

She has seen *Giselle*, who is loved for a day by the prince. When he foresakes her for a princess, Giselle goes crazy.

She has seen *The Story of Three Loves*. The beautiful young ballerina dances for the artist she loves, even though she knows she has a weak heart and it will kill her. But she does it for him, to help him through an artistic block.

She asks for the *Nutcracker Suite* for Christmas. The father obliges. Six 78 rpms.

She puts on her ballet slippers, puts on side one, and prepares to dance. But instead of flutes and piccolos, there come a banging of tin, a kind of hiccuping, and a bunch of high-pitched voices singing

> *Dja ever see a tin flute dancing?*
> *Nothing is so funny as a hunka tin.*

She bursts into tears. It is Spike Jones's version, and there is hardly any music at all. The father tells her not to be silly. The record is a marriage of two great arts — music and humor.

Bill Haley and his Comets come to town. Also Freddy Bell and the Bellboys. The son gets tickets and buys the record. He wants to know all the words of "Rock Around the Clock" and perfect his jitterbugging so that he can get up and dance in the aisles at the concert.

He puts the record on repeat and sits beside the record player all morning, writing down the words. He says he doesn't mind practicing certain steps with his sister, since she is at least a better partner than his dressing gown cord hooked around the bed post.

The daughter falls in love with a young man who can pompom *The Barber of Seville* from start to finish. He can sing the "Freude, schoener Goetterfunken" from Beethoven's Ninth, and he knows all the *Carmina Burana* in Medieval Latin.

He takes her home with him to listen to his record collection.

She chooses *Petrouchka*, planning to tell him about the doll with the heart. He puts on *Turandot*. Then he sits up and sings "Nessun dorma," pounding on the arm of the couch with his fist.

Next he plays *The Song of the Earth* and sings along with Fischer-Dieskau about the glowing knife in his breast.

The daughter gets home at two o'clock.

The father asks where the hell she's been and what the hell she's been doing. She tells him she has been listening to records.

The daughter falls in love with another man who can read the newspaper, eat a sandwich, talk on the telephone, watch television, and memorize songs on the radio almost simultaneously, or at least in quick succession.

She waits for the TV commercials to tell him something. But he also likes commercials and can sing most of them.

After the 11:30 movie, he turns up the radio and reads a back issue of the *New Yorker.* She curls up beside him. He is reading the history of the orange. She takes the magazine from him and tells him he's the only one. He closes his eyes, smiles, and nods his head. He reaches out his arm and turns up the volume on the radio and sings

> *If you can't be with the one you love*
> *Love the one you're with.*

He snaps his fingers to the beat. Next he sings

> *Bye, bye, Miss American Pie*

and falls asleep.

WEDDING

This is the story of a wedding and a wedding night. I wanted to wear a lovely nightgown on my wedding night. I wanted to be the loveliest, most desirable woman my husband had ever seen. I wanted him not to recognize me on my wedding night. I wanted him to look up in surprise and delight when he saw me in my nightgown and ask: How can this wonderful woman be the plain, dull, everyday girl I thought I was marrying, who stayed in my room secretly after visiting hours and shared my bed, loving me silently and fearing all the time we would be discovered?

I searched for a gown to transform me and please him. I fingered the nightgowns of Fifth Avenue. Then I went to the bargain basements of West 34th. And there I found my nightgown. It was delicate cotton, striped blue and white. It lay entangled in a mass of mark-downs, among nylon tiger and leopard patterns, purple pajamas with feathers, and soiled baby dolls.

The label on my nightgown read: Designed for Intrigue, a division of Exquisite Industries. I held it against me and knew I had to have it. It was topless.

An old sales lady, a crone with a brown tooth, loped up to me. "He'll love it," she said and frowned at the same time. She fished in the lingerie on the table and found a little pink jacket.

"This goes with it," she said. Then she winked and laughed. "But you'll never use it. He'll never let you put it on because he'll be too busy taking the rest off."

The customer next to me, a man who was holding a

nightgown with brown and black leopard spots, turned to look at me, first at my face and then at my breasts. Then he turned back to the leopard gown, which had slits from the armpit to the ankle.

My nightgown cost eight dollars.

After the wedding ceremony and the cake and the Champagne, we went to a friend's apartment, six of us: my husband and I, my husband's roommate, the friend whose apartment it was, a girl my husband had gone to college with but who was never his girl friend, or so he said, and her husband. She had come all the way from Washington with her husband especially for our wedding.

The roommate had prepared a special spaghetti dinner for us. We sat with plates of spaghetti on our laps. I thought: You are married now and this is your first meal with your husband. I felt warm and benign, even radiant. Our suitcase with my nightgown in it stood by the door.

I sat with my plate of spaghetti on my knees, and I kept my head bowed, looking at the plate sitting on my white dress, a fancy tablecloth, and I wondered if I could get a knife and fork and a glass of wine on this tablecloth, beside the plate, and stay still enough not to disturb or upset anything.

My husband had difficulty eating because he had burned his lip. He said "Ouch" and "Ow" every now and then. The night before he had gone to the Village with some friends to bid farewell to bachelorhood. He burned his lip with a cigarette at Your Father's Mustache. By the next day his lip had swollen, and it hurt him to smile. The burn showed as a dark spot in the wedding photographs.

The roommate said: "Do you think China will get into the United Nations?"

And someone said: "Well, I happen to be in a position to know for certain that . . ."

And someone else said: "You're dead wrong because it . . ."

And my husband said: "If this country would only . . ."

And the girl who was never a girl friend said: "Even if it did you'd still have the problem of . . ."

I remembered not to forget to call my mother.

I noticed I had spilled two drops of marinara sauce on my wedding dress. It was the prettiest dress I had ever owned. I bought it for forty dollars at Franklin and Simon. It was fine white netting with white woolen flowers embroidered all over. It had long sleeves and came to just above my knees. When I tried it on I felt tall and slim and lovely. I bought a new white bra and new white panties with a flower design to wear under my beautiful dress.

The morning of my wedding I got dressed very slowly. I was alone. I stood before the mirror that rested on the dresser and looked at my face and the top half of my dress. Then I stood on a chair before the mirror to see the lower half. I was worried about my knees. My brother called them potato knees. I said to my knees in the mirror: Just pretend you're going to a costume party, and you're going as a pretty girl. It's only a costume party. It'll be fun. I met my husband at a costume party, after all. I wore a black mask and just an ordinary dress. But he fell in love with me. He said he liked the way I danced.

On the morning of my wedding I was ready too soon and they were late coming to get me. I sat and waited and watched the snow coming down.

They came for me and took me to a little room next to the room of the wedding. My husband stood in a corner and nodded when I came in. I saw the burn on his lip. He turned his head away. He's nervous, I thought, and I smiled at him. I looked around for someone to tell me how pretty I looked. But everyone was busy. Someone was writing the zip code after the return address on our wedding announcements. Someone adjusted the carnation in his coat. Someone offered my husband a cigarette. Which he declined.

The men went into the wedding room first, and I was left with the photographer. He photographed me close-up looking out the window at the snow. Then he backed away for a full-length. I smiled. The photographer lowered his camera and made a silent whistle, shaking his head.

"You're the first bride I've ever seen in a mini-skirt," he said.

So that was why no one said anything. That was why my husband could not look at me. They are all ashamed of me. How can I go in there to be married in this dress, with my potato knees? Dear God, what can I do? The last time I wore a dress that was too short was at my father's funeral. It was the only black dress I owned. I had made it myself when I worked as a salesgirl one summer. They let me go right through the service and then, just before it was my turn to place the flowers on the grave, my aunt said: "Don't you think your dress is a little too short for a funeral?" I wanted to die.

The photographer said: "Aren't you going in?" Then someone came to get me. "What are you waiting for?" this person said and led me into the room where the people waited. I held my breath and walked across the green carpet, before their eyes, and stood next to my husband. "I thought you weren't coming," he whispered, and I could not tell if he was joking or angry or hopeful.

And we were married.

I thought I would wear my wedding dress often afterwards and tell people this was the dress I wore to get married. But just a few weeks later, as we drove through France, the suitcase with my dress was stolen. I cried. I looked in flea markets and thrift shops for my dress in every town we came to. I still look for the girl who must be wearing my wedding dress with the red marinara spots. When I see her I shall go to her and ask her to give it back, for sentimental reasons.

I still have the panties with the flower design, however. The nylon has grayed and the elastic has gone. They are in an old laundry bag waiting to be used as a dust rag.

I ate my spaghetti and I ate my salad.

"You have only to compare the situation in South Africa . . . but the French in Algeria finally learned that . . . and the Russians of course are another matter altogether . . . well not altogether, look at it this way . . ."

I wondered what a good wife would do: Sit smiling and show a lively interest in the topic under discussion; sit without smiling and eat; try to change the subject; or go and lie down in the next room. I did not know the answer. I had only been married for two hours.

So I told myself: How fortunate you are to be sitting here in this room where clever things are being stated. How fortunate you are to be a bride sitting here eating spaghetti and listening to clever people, one of whom is your husband.

Between salad and dessert I went to the bathroom. Between dessert and coffee I went to the kitchen for a glass of water. After coffee I checked the suitcase to make sure my nightgown was there. I reminded myself, again, not to forget the phone call.

"You and I met at the wrong time," said the girl, who was never a girl friend, to my husband.

The roommate looked across to where I was bent over the suitcase, to see if I had heard. The girl's husband from Washington was in the bathroom.

I went and stood by my husband and put my hand on his shoulder. It was firm and comforting.

"If I were the government of South Viet Nam . . ." he said.

I squeezed his shoulder, meaning shouldn't we be going now.

"But you're not the government," the girl said, "and if you were you'd find that . . ."

I smiled and squeezed my husband's shoulder again and said into his ear: "Don't you think . . . ?"

"I would tell the Americans," he said.

"But that would run directly against your interests," said the girl.

I thought I would go and lie down on the bed in the next

room. But the roommate was looking at me and his eyes said: How are you going to be able to satisfy the brain of such a brilliant man in the years to come?

So I sat down again, and listened, leaning forward and nodding, and I said every now and then: "That's a good point," or "There's more to it than that, don't you think?"

My husband looked at his watch and said: "Good God, why didn't you tell me?" and we stood up to go.

"But the phone call," I said. And we called my mother long distance to tell her that all had gone well. We also told her the cake was delicious, and we passed the receiver to the others so that they, too, could tell her.

Three women had prepared the cake. My mother and her neighbors, Mrs. Hamilton and Mrs. Wilson. It was a rich, dark fruitcake. My mother bought the ingredients and mixed them together. The cake was baked in Mrs. Hamilton's oven, for it could be relied upon to maintain an even temperature. When the cake was baked it was taken across the road to Mrs. Wilson, who had a special recipe for marzipan icing. Her marzipan looked like fine alabaster. She spent the whole afternoon icing the cake for she always had time on her hands.

They packed the cake in a cake tin and tied it in a closely fitting cotton bag and mailed it to me. Inside the tin was a note: We wish you a wonderful journey through the future. Love is a wonderful thing. Mother, Mrs. Hamilton, Mrs. Wilson.

On the morning of my wedding they came to take the cake to the room where I would be married. The cake was a square slab. It weighed five pounds. They carried it on a plywood board covered with aluminum foil. They had to transport it only a few blocks, but on the way the car skidded and the cake fell to the floor of the car. The icing was cracked. To cover this fault line they took small white chrysanthemum blooms from the flower vase in the corner and laid them across the top of the cake.

When I walked into the room in my white dress and saw the cake with flowers, I wondered why it looked like a little square grave.

We kept a piece of the cake. We took it home to our apartment and wrapped it in foil and put it in the freezer compartment. Our friends said we should keep it until the birth of our first child. After two years I took the cake from the freezer and unwrapped it and held it for a moment. Then I threw it away. My husband asked me why I had thrown it out without even tasting it. I told him it had defrosted and refrozen so many times in the course of the years that it would be dangerous to eat it. He nodded.

We still have a photograph of the cake, with the flowers, and whenever anyone gets out the wedding photographs we tell them how it was made and what happened to it. It makes a good story, especially the part about patching up the crack.

"Can we drop you off?" said the girl who was never a girl friend.

My husband said: "Are you sure it won't be out of your way?" He whispered into her ear where we were going, for I was not to know. It was to be my surprise. The girl and her husband drove us across the park and down Park Avenue to the Waldorf.

We got out and thanked them and they said: "Have a good night, but don't be too good."

We were led to the honeymoon suite, which had an enormous bed and long mirrors along one wall.

"This is a lovely surprise," I said. I went into the bathroom to put on my blue nightgown with the pink jacket.

"Look," I said. And he looked and smiled and said: "That's very nice." He had turned on the television set and was changing channels with one hand.

"It's your surprise," I said. I went and sat next to him on the bed and began to unbutton my pink jacket to show him what a

71

special nightgown it was.

"*Wuthering Heights* with Laurence Olivier," he said.

"I've seen it," I said. "Years ago, when I was still in high school. I fell in love with Heathcliff."

"Would you mind terribly if we watched it now, I've never seen it?" he said.

"Of course I don't mind," I said.

We sat together in bed and watched the movie. It was the first time I had ever had a television set in my bedroom and watched a movie in bed. During a commercial I went to stand by the mirror to see if my nightgown really looked lovely, or if I had made a mistake. I wished I had bought the leopard pattern with the slits instead.

When the movie was over we phoned our breakfast order to the desk. Then we turned out the light and lay back in bed.

My husband stretched and groaned. "I'm really tired," he said. Then he looked at me and saw that I wanted to make love. We did.

The next morning a steward in a white jacket brought breakfast on a serving cart. The bacon and eggs and toast lay on silver serving platters under silver domes. The breakfast cost eight dollars. The same as my nightgown. I still have the nightgown. But the sales lady was wrong. I always wear it with the pink jacket.

MARGUERITE

When we arrived at the house it was dusk, a brown dusk unlike the gray and blue of the coast.

Marguerite was sitting on the front porch. She sat astride a little wooden bench, mixing something on a large slab of black slate, which rested on the bench between her knees. She watched our approach.

"Doesn't she look marvelous?" Neil said as we drove up to the house. "Always wears slacks. Only woman her age I know who can get away with it."

He stopped the car with a jerk next to the Jeep and the old Harley Davidson motorcycle, and he jumped out and ran up to Marguerite. She did not stop mixing. She held the slab with one hand and a flat piece of wood with the other. She sat there and watched Neil run to her across the strip of dry lawn, and I saw that she was the kind of person whose lips did not part when she smiled.

Neil knelt on one knee beside her and put his arms around her. He kissed her on both cheeks. He drew his head back from her face and looked at her, and then kissed her again on both cheeks. Marguerite did not stop mixing, but she closed her eyes as Neil kissed her. As far as I could see, they did not say anything to each other.

Neil sat down at the other end of Marguerite's bench and beckoned to me to come. I got out of the car and walked over to them. I stopped before the porch about four feet in front of them.

"See, Marguerite, there she is, what do you think?" Neil said.

Marguerite looked at me. "I could feel that you were coming today. That's why I'm doing this messy work on the front porch, so that I could see you come. Forgive me for not stopping this pest of a task for a moment or so. I'm mixing an ochre for a new urn I'm making. And if I stop now it'll be ruined."

"Still the same Marguerite," Neil said. "Always doing something original. So creative and artistic. Wait till you see her handiwork. You'll love it. Best taste of any woman I know."

"That's not the thing to say in front of your bride," Marguerite said and bent her thin mouth in a smile. "Besides, it's inaccurate. It is she who has the best taste."

She held the slate at an angle, to catch the last rays of the sun. "There. That's just about it." She motioned to me to step up onto the porch beside her. She got up from the bench and stood beside me. She was only a little shorter than I, but when she reached up and held my chin and turned my head this way and that, looking at my face, I felt extraordinarily large and awkward. I stepped back a pace, away from her. Marguerite drew close to me again. "Those bones," she said to Neil. She outlined my chin and cheeks with her finger.

I wanted Marguerite to like me. All the way from the coast over the mountains to her property I had concentrated on her and prepared myself for spending several days with her in the western plains.

But when she stood so close and held my chin I had to step away from her. And in stepping back I knocked the slate with the ochre mixture off the porch. It landed face down on the grass.

"Watch out," said Neil. "God, look what you've done." And he jumped down from the porch and picked up the piece of slate. A yellowish circle of paint stained the beige grass. Neil stood there below us, the slab in his hand, his face a pale triangle.

Marguerite bent down and took the slab from his hand. She

hurled it over his head, and it smashed into several pieces on the gravel driveway beyond the car.

"One afternoon's work in the context of a lifetime is meaningless," she said. And she turned and went into the house.

Neil got our bags from the car. I waited for him on the porch. Marguerite's house was one of the oldest in the country. It had been one of the first to be built after the road over the mountains had been opened up. Marguerite's good taste in restoring and maintaining it had often been described to me by Neil. She had scraped away old paint, turned floorboards, and oiled every wooden surface she could find with her own blend of oils. She had got up on the roof and painted the old iron with a maroon rust-proof paint. She had got down on her knees and crawled under the house to slap creosote on the wooden foundations. She baked her own bread, used a potter's wheel, drove a tractor and rode a motorcycle, and shot crows. She had also designed the wrought-iron trellises for the honeysuckle and wisteria that smothered the porches of her house.

I knew both the house and Marguerite intimately, before I had seen either.

"Everyone who meets her just loves her, instantly," Neil had told me often. "Her grandmother was French, of course, and it certainly shows. An oasis of civilization in the middle of all that back of beyond and nobody worthwhile around for hundreds of miles. But she says that the people she really likes always come to her."

"And what about Mr. Marguerite?" I had asked when Neil first told me about her. "What does he say?"

"Who? Oh, you mean Angus?" Neil shrugged. "A grand chap. He's still working on Marguerite's genealogy, I shouldn't wonder. Last time Marguerite mentioned it he'd gone back almost as far as Charlemagne. He adores her. They're just like newlyweds, after twenty years of marriage. You wait till you see how Angus has rigged out the annex Marguerite built for him. It's his den. Fantastic."

Inside the house the air was dark brown and black and very cool. All the windows were shut and the blinds and curtains drawn. The night outside was bright compared with the inside of Marguerite's house. My eyes took some time to adjust to the gloom.

Marguerite turned to me. "When the inside of the house matches the night, then it is time to open the windows and curtains and blinds and doors and let in the cool night air. When the inside of the house matches the dawn, then it is time to close everything up again, to block out the heat of the day."

"Neil talks about you all the time," I said.

"He has been more than a son to me," she said.

Neil crashed into the room with the suitcases. "Is it good to be back here again!" he said, dumping the cases in the middle of the kitchen floor. He went and stood beside Marguerite and put his arm about her shoulders. "She's a wonderful person, isn't she?" he said to me. "Just as I promised you."

Marguerite pulled away from him. "I've given you two my bedroom. You know where to go, Neil. Take your bride and let her revive a little."

"But what about you?" Neil said. "Honestly, we don't want to put you out. We can sleep anywhere."

Marguerite dismissed his offer. She opened the top half of the kitchen door and held up her hand.

She was a brown woman. Like a nut. And she matched the air and countryside of the plains. I would never match this region, except possibly during a rainstorm.

Marguerite went through the house pulling back the curtains. Neil took me to the bedroom. He was almost skipping as he walked.

He kissed me and began to make love to me on the white, hand-stitched coverlet of Marguerite's bed.

"Time to open up the windows in here. You'll need all the cool air you can get," Marguerite said, poking her head around the door. "And I need your help in the kitchen, both of you."

Neil rolled off the bed and sprang to his feet, holding his shirt in front of him.

Marguerite smiled. "I'd appreciate your folding back the bedspread first," she said.

"What? Oh, of course, just about to, yes, certainly," said Neil.

We sat around the wooden table in the kitchen. While Marguerite poured us glasses of wine, Neil shelled peas and I diced the mangoes and pawpaw we had brought. I worked slowly, for I suddenly did not care for their smell, their rich orange color, and their texture. Marguerite stood near Neil and talked to him. They talked without stopping and so quickly that I felt I was following a foreign language. Once when I looked up I found Marguerite looking at me.

"Forgive us," she said. "I don't often get a chance to talk to an old friend. It can be lonely out here."

Angus appeared for dinner. We all had roast pork, except Angus, who had a grilled lamb chop.

"Good old Angus," said Neil. "Just the same as ever. If it's not a lamb chop it's beefsteak."

"Or a lean beef sausage," said Angus. "It makes for continuity. And continuity is something we don't have enough of these days. Isn't that so, my dear?" He looked across the table at Marguerite.

Marguerite nodded and smiled at him and reached over and held his hand. Angus looked like an old, old man.

"Wipe your chin now, pet," Marguerite said to her husband. "And then it's time for dessert. A lovely fruit salad."

There was nothing on Angus's chin that I could see, but he wiped it with his napkin, going right into the corners of his mouth and out as far as his ears. Neil also wiped his mouth and chin.

"My project," Angus then said, "is to provide a sense of continuity, expecially for our Marguerite. She goes back to Charlemagne, you know. French. I hope to get her back to the Gauls, you know. Come, I'll show you."

Marguerite held him back as he made to get up. "We haven't finished dinner, pet. And after dessert it's your bedtime. You can show us your project tomorrow." She turned to Neil and me. "He has correspondence from all over the world, and newspaper clippings, and old churchyard records. One wall of the annex is completely covered by a chart, starting with me and Angus at the bottom. He has to stand on a set of steps to reach Charlemagne." She turned to Angus. "Isn't that so?"

Neil laughed with approval. "You're terrific, Angus."

That night I asked Neil when we would be going back. He told me we would leave in a couple of days. But after four days we were still there. After dinner on the fourth day Neil sighed and said to Marguerite that he supposed it was time for us to be thinking of returning. Marguerite wanted to know what the hurry was. She said she would be hurt and offended if we left so soon.

On the fifth night I begged Neil to tell her that we would leave the following day. I said we had outstayed our welcome, we had a lot to do when we got back home, and I did not care for the air of the plains, which made Neil ruffle my hair and call me crazy. I remained quiet for some time, then I asked Neil why Marguerite was keeping Angus locked up in the annex.

"What on earth do you mean?" he said. And he laughed.

"He's a prisoner," I said.

"Marguerite is a good woman," Neil said. "I thought that would be apparent to you by now."

Marguerite, Neil, and I did everything together. The only time we saw Angus was in the evening at the dinner table. It was the only time that he left the annex built for him by Marguerite. During the hour or two that we saw him he looked only at Marguerite. When dinner was over she told him to be sure to pay a visit to the bathroom before he went to bed.

On the sixth day Neil and I drove the Jeep, following Marguerite on her motorcycle across the fields, in and out of the shallow valleys and along the dry stream beds, to the banks of a river. Marguerite rode the motorcycle as if it were a horse. She said that it was the one exciting thing she did, although the cycle was getting badly shaken up and could fall to bits any time. We spread an old army disposal blanket on the river bank under a willow tree. We ate a little, drank some wine. Then I walked through the field of knee-high grass that sloped up from the river. At the ridge, in the sun, I came across a nest of brown and yellow snakes. And I screamed. The snakes slid away into the grass.

I had never screamed like that before. The sensation in my throat was new, I screamed again.

Neil sprang to his feet. He had been lying on his back under the willow with Marguerite. He ran up the slope toward me. I found myself moaning and sobbing. He stood beside me and put his arms around me.

"Hey, what the heck is the matter?"

I moaned and whimpered. He shook me.

"For God's sake, tell me."

"Snakes."

He made an impatient sound with his tongue. "Of course you'll see snakes around here. What do you expect at this time of year?"

I started to cry again. Neil shook me. "Did it bite you? For God's sake, answer."

He sat me on the ground and unfolded the blade of his camp knife, which had been hanging from his belt waiting for an emergency ever since we had arrived.

"No," I said.

Neil led me back down the slope to Marguerite, who was half-sitting half-lying on the blanket. She poured herself another glass of wine.

Neil dropped me on the blanket in front of her.

"Snake," he said.

I could tell from the way the corners of her mouth strained to stay in a straight line that she wanted to laugh. And I knew that behind her sunglasses her eyes were beginning to crinkle into little slits of laughter.

I stood up. "It was nothing. I'm just a bit tired. I think I'll drive back to the house."

I paused for a second, to feel whether Neil would come with me or stay with Marguerite.

"It's still so early," he said. "And it's the worst time of day. Better to wait until it cools down a bit."

I backed away from them. "So long."

Neil had sat down on the blanket. "You're okay on your own, driving?"

I walked carelessly away from them. And as I walked along the river bank to the clearing where we had left the vehicles I heard Marguerite burst into laughter.

I took the Jeep and left the motorcycle for them.

At nine o'clock Marguerite and Neil had not returned. Angus emerged and sat down at the dinner table. I placed his food before him.

"Such a rewarding day," he said. "Vercingetorix was a most interesting fellow. And what about you? Did you have an entertaining day?"

"Most entertaining," I replied. "Neil and Marguerite must have decided to camp out. It's such a lovely night."

Angus raised his eyebrows a little. He began to frown. Then his forehead smoothed over again.

"Isn't there something on my chin that should be wiped off?" He looked right into my face.

I grabbed his arm. "I am not your Marguerite."

He drew his arm away and wiped his chin. He pushed back his chair. "I don't think I'll wait for dessert. I'm feeling a bit tired, and I think I'll just go straight to bed." At the door he added, "And of course I'll make a stop by the bathroom first, so don't worry about me. And tell the youngsters when they come that they are quite welcome to stay on as long as they wish."

After the bathroom Angus poked his head around the door again. He held a hurricane lamp in his hand. "Actually I think I'll just go and look for them. I don't like them out there alone at night. Anything could happen.'' And off he went, across the grass, walking slowly, his lamp held out in front of him, his eyes on the ground, as if he were looking for a button or something small that had dropped.

I went through the house opening the curtains and the windows. Then I sat on the front porch, watching the sky turn black. I fell asleep sitting there, and at dawn the sound of the Harley Davidson woke me up. I watched its headlight draw closer.

Marguerite and Neil came to a stop at the end of the drive. Neil was sitting behind Marguerite, his arms around her waist. He got off and waited beside her while she fiddled with the Harley, getting it positioned so that the stand would not sink into the gravel. They had not looked at me. Then they walked across the grass toward me.

I sat there and watched them both come to me and stand in front of the porch. They had to look up at me.

''Engine trouble,'' said Neil, and he looked away. ''What a night. You're the lucky one to have come back early.''

I did not answer him. ''Angus has escaped,'' I told Marguerite. ''He's searching for you.''

Marguerite sighed. She looked tired, and I wished I had tried to stop Angus going off. But I had been too angry at everything. Marguerite left Neil beside me. It was as if she were handing him over, transferring him to my care. Then she went back to the Jeep. ''I'll be back when I've got him. Shouldn't take too long,'' she said.

''I think we'll be going back today,'' I called back.

Marguerite nodded and drove off.

It was the seventh day. Poor weak Neil was mine again, and Marguerite was out retrieving her Angus. For the first time I saw that Marguerite and I had a lot in common.

SUMMER IN FRANCE

There was a summer when the wasps were particularly bad. Every morning when Lark slipped and clattered down the cobbled lane to the bakery, several wasps followed her, attracted to her yellow dress and drawn along in her wake. If she ran from them, they teemed after her and bumped into her when she stopped. They terrified her.

Lark was hating this summer in France. She thought she might be pregnant, but could not find a way to tell Tom. He was always talking to someone else, or reading. He no longer seemed to talk to her or look at her, although she felt she was essential to him, like the paper that is wrapped around a bowl and tucked into the crevices when the bowl is packed in a box.

Tom often sat with his arm around her or his hand resting on her knee while he talked animatedly to Elizabeth or Jean-Claude. If Lark listened, beyond Giscard d'Estaing this and Pompidou that and Mitterand something else, she sometimes learned things about her husband. She learned that he loved the fireside scene in *Women in Love* and the novels of Herman Hesse. At breakfast the other morning she learned that he had made himself ill when he was ten by frying and eating a dozen eggs when he came home from school one day and found his mother not home.

But most of his stories she had heard dozens of times, intimate stories that he told to new acquaintances, using the same words, the same phrases, the same pauses each time. There was nothing for her to add or say. Once, before they married, she had said that Charles de Gaulle resembled Willy Brandt, and

Tom had demanded that she explain what she meant. She said she couldn't really, and Tom told her to hold her tongue if she did not know what she was talking about. His fury had frightened her. When they got back home she was going to get her Ph.D. in history or politics to make herself altogether more interesting, to make it possible for her to speculate on the outcome of elections, to make Tom want to listen when she spoke.

Lark read the newspapers, but the stories she remembered were the fillers, the items about the Indiana woman who crawled and rolled through the snow with two broken legs after her car had run off the road, and the lady from Toledo, Ohio, who took a taxi to San Francisco. And now she was reading wasp stories. That morning she had read of a man who inhaled one. The wasp stung his throat, the throat swelled, blocked off his windpipe, and the man died.

To get to the bakery she had to steel herself. She walked deliberately, with her hand over her mouth and nose, breathing slowly and quietly. Clustered about the bakery door were more wasps, and inside the display windows, crawling over the fruit tarts and the sugared breads, more. The girls behind the counter did not seem to care. They chatted and laughed with their mouths wide open, moving the breads and cakes and flicking at the wasps. Lark remained outside in the square until the crowd of customers in the bakery had thinned. She watched the ancient slate-green Rhone. In the middle was a flat rock where a king had once ordered a table and banquet to be set. He sat on the rock and feasted, with the water swirling by. And he watched while one of the servants bringing him food drowned.

"Good morning," the girls behind the counter sang when she walked in. "What can we give you today?"

As if they did not know. Every morning she asked for eight rolls, two for each of them, but by the time breakfast had been set on the terrace at the back under the grapevine, the wasps had found their way up the front of the house and over the top and were swarming about them as they sat down.

If a wasp alighted on the butter or fell into the milk jug, Lark ate her roll without butter and took her coffee without milk. She had read that a startled wasp deposited its sting in fright, and that once deposited in food, the sting retained its poison for some time.

She spent most meals walking about the little terrace, turning away from the wasps and smuggling every mouthful to her mouth. Tom and Jean-Claude laughed at her. Her behavior irritated them.

"If you move they'll follow you even more," Jean-Claude said. He sat impervious, the brown-and-yellow striped bodies coasting about his head.

"You'll get an ulcer if you spend every meal on your feet," Tom informed her. "Relax, enjoy yourself."

"Women rarely get ulcers," Elizabeth said. She never looked at anyone when she spoke, because she had to keep her eye on her new baby.

But Tom looked at Elizabeth and listened to her. They had gone to college together, and then Elizabeth had married a Frenchman, which seemed to be as good as getting a Ph.D. in that it made her more interesting to Tom than an ordinary woman.

There was nowhere for Lark to go to get away from the wasps. The fig trees and vegetable garden made the next terrace, set into the hillside above the house, impossible. Indoors was just as bad. With the shutters open, the wasps flew freely in and out, hovering over the fruit bowl, the sink, and even the bathroom fixtures.

Sometimes, when the others were busy outside, she could close the shutters and doors and stay in the house.

One morning, before the others awakened, Lark took ten empty beer bottles and placed an inch of sugar and water in the bottom of each. She stowed the bottles at intervals around the terrace, behind rocks and plants and other objects to keep them out of sight. Then, as she stood and watched, wasps flew to the bottles and crawled inside and fell into the sweet water. She planned to empty out the dead wasps every morning and refill the bottles with sugar and water.

Lark was washing her hair over the stone sink in the kitchen. Tom and Jean-Claude sat outside and watched Elizabeth bathe the baby. She had cleared the breakfast things and placed a blue plastic bathtub on the table on the terrace.

From the kitchen Lark could overhear everything they said. And she could see them if she raised her head. Tom watched the child in the tub. Then he stood up and wet his hands in the bath water and lathered them with soap and tickled the baby all over. Elizabeth ran inside to get her camera. Jean-Claude laughed.

When Elizabeth had taken the photo and finished bathing the child, she wrapped him in a towel and handed him to Tom. Then Jean-Claude asked Tom why he and Lark did not settle down and have a family.

"Plenty of time," said Tom and shrugged and laughed. "Things are fine as they are. Why change it? And who needs kids?"

"You'd enjoy being a father," Elizabeth said. She went and stood by Jean-Claude, her hand on his shoulder. Together they watched their child on Tom's knee.

"Time enough for all that," Tom said. He held the child above his head and made him laugh.

Lark watched Elizabeth take another photo. Elizabeth was one of the prettiest women she knew.

They sat by the river and ate fried fish and fresh melon. In the dusk the wasps had thinned out, and those that still flew about had become more attracted to the street lamp behind them. The baby slept, covered with mosquito netting.

"If life could always be like this," Elizabeth said. Jean-Claude rubbed the back of her neck.

Tom told a story. "This reminds me of the night I liberated myself," he said. Elizabeth, and Jean-Claude leaned forward, interested. But Lark had heard this one many times. She sat quietly and ate the little fish.

"You've no idea what a simple gesture can do to free you from the pressures and hypocrisies of a lifetime," Tom said. "It happened one night. There were eight of us. Two of them were young priests. We had cooked a steak over an open fire and eaten it with bread and salad and wine—just a cheap local wine with a pull-off cap, no cork. We sat around the fire. Everyone was in a good mood. We sat or lay in the grass. A bit like now. Then suddenly I knew what I had to do. I stood up and took off my clothes, and I jumped over the fire. Then everyone stood up and threw off their clothes, and we held hands and danced around the fire. Those of us who dared jumped over it. Everyone except the priests. They just sat there, in their clothes, looking a bit uncomfortable. But they still sat there, watching, taking everything in. They could have walked away if they had wanted to. They didn't have to watch. We had a ball. We jumped and ran and horsed around. It's the most natural thing in the world, to go about naked. Here we all were, just jumping about and laughing. There's nothing to it, just taking each other's bodies for granted. The guys tried to jump on one of the girls and make it with her, a Norwegian blonde. She led everyone on but she wasn't having any."

Elizabeth turned to Lark. "And where were you when all this was happening? Did you liberate yourself?"

Lark shook her head. Tom laughed. "She'd gone home early, to bed," he said. "She missed out on everything. God, you'll never know. It's the most natural thing in the world. Everyone's so hung up about nudity."

Lark counted the number of little fish heads left on her plate. She had eaten thirty-two while Tom told his story. Jean-Claude paid for the meal while Tom was still fumbling in his pocket for his money. Lark felt ill.

They decided to go swimming. There was a stream, a tributary of the river, some ten miles south of the house. Just before the stream joined the river it made a sharp turn. On one side of the turn the water ran deep and swift, swirling against a bank of sheer rock. On the other side the current was slow and edged its way around a deposit of sand, forming a small beach.

Lark put on her bathing suit and joined the others outside the house.

"Your swimsuit's too small for you," Tom said. "It must be all these rolls and bread and nothing to do."

Elizabeth and Jean-Claude turned to look.

"Stop it, Tom. It's fine," Elizabeth said. "There won't be many people at the beach anyway."

"It won't hold," said Tom. "She's had it for years. The hook at the back will snap as soon as she starts to swim."

He was right. The suit was old.

"I could wear nothing if it snaps," Lark said.

"Don't be silly," said Tom.

"I have a second suit I could lend you," said Elizabeth in a kind voice.

"It wouldn't fit her," said Tom.

Lark shrugged. "It doesn't matter. I probably won't go swimming anyway. I have a book I want to read."

Tom put his arm around her shoulders. "That's solved, then. Let's go."

"You can read out loud to the baby," said Elizabeth. "He loves women's voices."

When they got there the sun was high overhead and slightly to the south. There were about twenty people on the beach, in the water, and diving from the rock face on the opposite bank.

Jean-Claude and Tom ran straight to the water. When he was halfway down the beach Tom came running back and kissed Lark. "Sure you're okay?" he asked, and then ran back to Jean-Claude in the water.

Elizabeth fussed about setting things right for the baby. She spread a padded plastic sheet on the sand and on the sheet a white towel. She placed the child on his stomach on the towel and then she fiddled with a parasol so that its shade fell over the baby's body. Over the parasol she draped mosquito netting, which she anchored with shoes and bags and some stones at the edge of the plastic.

She stood back and admired the construction. "That should keep him safe," she said.

Jean-Claude and Tom called to her from the water. They splashed each other to show her how wonderful it was.

"Are you sure you don't mind staying with the baby?"

"Of course not."

"But are you sure?" she persisted. "It seems a shame."

"I'm happy to read."

"Well, all right, if you're sure," said Elizabeth, backing away toward the water and tucking her hair into her cap. "If he cries, give him the juice in the bottle with the blue cap."

Lark watched Elizabeth run into the water, where Tom hoisted her on his shoulders. Lark drew her knees under her chin and sat hunched with her book before her. She wore a sunhat and sunglasses to protect her face and neck, and draped towels around her back and arms and knees. The wasps flew about, attracted to the garbage cans and to the people.

Lark had only to move her eyes, without moving her head, to see the baby. He was asleep on the white towel. His back moved in and out as he breathed. One or two wasps alighted on the white netting and crawled about.

One wasp was particularly methodical. She watched it crawl down from the highest point of the net tent and make its way along the edge of the netting at sand level. It crawled into the toe of Elizabeth's sandal and upon emerging at the heel found that the edge of the netting had been caught up by the buckle. The wasp slipped through the gap and into the tent. She watched it walk across the towel toward the baby's foot. Just before it reached the foot, she brought her book down on it and crushed

it through the netting. The parasol and net construction col-
lapsed and the baby woke up crying. Elizabeth hurried from
the water to comfort him.

Lark asked Tom if they could leave soon.

"What's the hurry?" he asked.

"The wasps," she said.

He laughed and gave her a hug.

They went to Vienne to buy a swimsuit for Lark. Tom stood
outside the changing room reading a book while Lark tried on
suits.

Then they all went on to eat nine courses on the terrace of a
three-star restaurant. Suddenly Tom pulled a dark red scarf out
of his coat pocket. It was not in any kind of wrapping, just
loose.

"A present for Lark," he said. He held the scarf by one corner and dangled it in front of her.

"When did you get that?" Lark asked.

"It's lovely," said Elizabeth.

"When you were trying on your swimsuit," Tom said.

Lark reached out for the scarf. He jerked it back, laughing.
"Say please," he said. And when she did not, he put the scarf
back in his pocket. The red corner poked out, and it looked as if
it were meant for him.

Back in the house Lark lay awake. Tom's coat, with the scarf
in its pocket, was across the back of the chair.

"You shoplifted the scarf, didn't you?" Lark said to Tom.

Tom laughed. He was furious. When he had finished laughing, he turned over and went to sleep.

When Lark returned from the bakery she heard Tom and
Elizabeth talking. Elizabeth held a postcard in her hand. "My
sister is coming," she told Tom. "If you stay until next week,
you'll meet her."

"Is she as beautiful as you?" Tom asked.

Elizabeth looked uncomfortable. "More beautiful," she replied, and she looked to see where Lark was. "Hi, Lark. Tom, here's Lark with the rolls." And Elizabeth ran over to Lark and led her to the table.

Jean-Claude was walking around the terrace, inspecting the grapevines and smiling off into the blue sky. He stood on a small rock pile. When he stepped back off the stones he kicked over one of the beer bottles.

"Good grief," he said. The bottle broke and several drowned wasps spilled onto the terrace. Then Jean-Claude went around the terrace collecting the other nine bottles. He lined them up in a row.

"Who on earth had the smart idea to put these everywhere?" He was angry. They all knew that Lark had done it.

"I wanted them to get into the bottles rather than have them bother us," Lark said.

"How stupid," Jean-Claude said. "They're attracting every wasp in the area, sending out invitations to a party." He made a rude noise and emptied all the bottles and put them in the garbage can, shaking his head the whole time.

"She meant well," Elizabeth said.

Tom laughed. "You just have to learn to live with minor nuisances like wasps," he told Lark.

Lark handed over the rolls and went inside. She leaned against the sink and watched them talking. Tom had broken his roll and was spreading it with butter and Elizabeth's home-made fig jam.

"Mussels, I love them, but I'm allergic," he said, starting off on another story.

A wasp landed on the piece of bread he held in his hand. It stuck in the jam.

"I ate them twice before I realized what it was."

Elizabeth smiled at her baby, nodding at Tom's story. Jean-Claude was reading the paper.

Tom gestured with his piece of bread. "I thought I was dy-ing. And I even wanted to die. Agony."

"I can't wear wool next to my skin," said Elizabeth.

The wasp was thoroughly coated in jam and was no longer moving.

"Maybe the mussels were rotten both times, and I'm not really allergic," said Tom. "But I'm not game to try them again to find out."

He opened his mouth to eat his bread and jam, but decided to finish his story. "Every time we go to a restaurant it's *moules* this and *moules* that. Delicious. But I can't eat 'em. It's hard."

Lark leaned forward over the sink. "Tom," she said quietly, "you'll die if you eat that piece of bread."

Tom laughed at her silliness and looked at Elizabeth for support. He put the slab of bread and butter and jam, with the wasp, in his mouth and chewed. Lark waited for him to notice the difference in texture and spit it all out. He swallowed. She waited for him to cry out and start to die.

Nothing happened.

Tom looked at her. "What's the matter with you, Lark? You're really saying crazy things."

"There was a wasp in your jam. You ate it." She was shouting at him.

"Nonsense," said Tom, frowning and shaking his head. He apologized to Elizabeth and Jean-Claude for her behavior.

"It might interest you to know that I'm pregnant," Lark shouted.

Tom laughed. "Aha. So that's it. That's what's the matter with you. Come here, Larkie, and gimme a kiss."

Lark stayed by the sink. Tom stayed sitting in his chair outside at the breakfast table, smiling and saying, "Well, well."

Elizabeth went in to Lark and put her arms around her. "That's wonderful news," she said, and brought Lark out to Tom.

A wasp that had been circling around the table seemed to be pushed off its course by the arrival of Elizabeth and Lark. It flew straight at Tom and landed on his collar. It crawled onto his neck. Lark screamed. Tom had felt the movement and clapped his hand to his neck. The wasp stung him.

Tom's neck and face swelled, and they rushed him to the doctor. The doctor told Tom he was allergic to the sting and the reaction would be much worse if he were stung again. He advised caution as far as wasps were concerned.

Tom was unable to talk for several days. He stayed in bed and was terrified the whole time that he was going to die. Later he said that if Lark had not screamed, it would not have happened.

Tom and Lark left France as soon as Tom felt he could travel. For some time after they got back Lark took care of him as if he were an invalid. They hardly spoke to each other anymore, even though Tom had his voice back. After a few months, when the wasp sting had already become another story, Tom left Lark, saying he had had enough, and some time after that, after their child was born, they divorced.

THE HOLLOW WOMAN

"We shall turn you into a princess," they told me. And they turned their backs as I undressed. But not quite, for they wanted to know what I was like.

"So white," they said when they saw me and forgot that they were not looking. "Just like a princess."

And then one of them pressed a thumb against my upper arm and marveled that that spot could turn even whiter. And at once they all started to prod my ribs and buttocks and thighs and wondered at the white-blue, and giggled, with one hand over the mouth.

Then they remembered themselves and shaded their faces with their hands.

They wrapped me in a patterned cloth, from my waist to my ankles. By winding it about me in a spiral they were able to make it so tight that my legs felt they had become one. They fastened the cloth at the waist with a cord and then took a strip of dark red cloth and bound it about my body, from my hips to my armpits. And then they put my arms into a jacket with long sleeves so close-fitting that I could move my arms only slightly.

Together they combed out my hair. They brought out several switches of hair, two and three feet long, and worked them together with my own brown hair into an intricate bun that sat heavily on the nape of my neck, pulling the hair directly back from my face so that the skin of my forehead and cheeks was taut. They brought out thick brown pencils and filled in the irregularities in my hairline. Until my face had become a perfect circle.

They brought heavy gold ornaments: a necklace, bracelets, a brooch for each shoulder, combs for my hair, and rings for every finger, with an especially elaborate ring for my right thumb. They pierced my earlobes and threaded ornate earrings through the holes. And on my feet they placed jeweled sandals with slender high heels.

They stood before me.

"How beautiful," they said.

With my skin so tight and my head so heavy, it was easy not to smile, and I acknowledged their praise by lowering my eyelids and looking at their feet.

"So refined," they said.

And they took me by the hands and led me into the garden.

The garden was close by. We had only to pass through one room, but because I was at the beginning, we probably moved more slowly than normal. And it must have taken some three or four minutes to reach the little gray bench under the frangipani tree in the garden.

I fixed my eyes on the tree to prevent it from disappearing, and I counted the blossoms and leaves with every step. Our bodies, slow and slender, scarcely disturbed the warm air as we walked. Their voices, softly praising my progress, drifted through the house and the garden, and were the only tangible mark of our presence.

I sat carefully on the bench in the shade beneath the tree. My hands rested neatly, one on each thigh, with all the fingers folded under.

They left me.

"Excellent," said a new voice.

I had thought I was alone in the garden. But at the sound of the voice I found that I did not turn suddenly. Nor did I cry out. I turned my head slowly to the right and felt my thickly knotted hair move across my neck.

A man sat at the end of the bench. He wore a long skirt of

brown and gray and blue and green. His skin was pale brown. His head was wrapped in a dark maroon cloth. He blended with the tree and the gravel and the bench.

"Excellent," he said again. Then he spoke to me at length.

The first lesson was to learn to stay without moving. I was quickly able to do this, and he praised me for my ready comprehension.

And I stayed very still in order to learn the second lesson, the lesson of words.

"There are three languages," he told me. "The first language is the middle language and is for those who are your equals. You will rarely use it. The second language is the low language and is for those who are beneath you in rank. Nearly everyone you meet will be beneath you. But you will never use the low language to them, for you may not confess your superiority before others. The third language is the high language and is for those whose rank is higher than yours. While no one is superior to you, you will mostly use the high language to show your humility and make others feel less uncomfortable about their inferiority.

"There are three conversations," he continued. "The first is the host conversation, to be used when you are in your own house and welcoming others. The second is the guest conversation, to be used when you are in the house of another. The third conversation is to be used when you are in transit and are neither host nor guest."

When I had learned the three conversations in each of the three languages, he told me I was equipped to begin the final and most difficult of lessons. He did not tell me the name of this third lesson.

We stood up and left the garden.

He led me to the room, and I sat on a chair on a platform raised six inches above the floor. Although I looked only past my knees to the floor before me, I could still see that many people had gathered outside and were pressing against the door and the windows waiting to enter. They came and stood before me, one by one, and I extended to each my right hand and bade him welcome, using the host conversation in the high language. Each one shook my hand and bowed low over it.

Thousands of people had come to offer me their greetings. After shaking my hand and completing the conversation, they moved on and made way for those who still crowded at the door and in the street outside.

I sat and welcomed each one.

When all had come and greeted me, my teacher told me I had completed the third lesson.

I was not certain what he meant, and I asked him the name of the lesson, using the high language. He told me to look at my right hand, resting on my thigh. And I did so.

When I saw my hand, I did not flinch or cry out. I observed my hand and understood my teacher. My fingers had swollen. So large had each finger become that it was clear I would be unable to remove the rings for several days.

I felt no pain.

My teacher said: "Had you cried out as your guests shook your hand and offered you their greeting, or had you removed the rings altogether before receiving your guests and shaking their hands, they would have been offended. They would have known that you were not a real princess, for princesses do not insult others, and they would have gone away."

He bathed my hand and informed me that I should now embark upon the journey.

Before I set out they came and removed most of my jewelry. "It is bad taste," they told me, "for a princess to travel dressed as a princess. It would make other people uncomfortable and ashamed."

They had to leave the rings on my right hand, however, and they also left the earrings in my ears. They instructed me to hide my hand under the end of my jacket as I traveled, for, in addition to sparing others embarrassment, I would also avoid those who coveted the possessions of others. And they warned me against moving my head, lest the earrings catch the light and attract attention.

When the train pulled in, it was already packed with thousands of people who had boarded long before me. So crowded was the train that it was impossible to enter through the doors. People were sitting on the steps and in the doorways. Several passengers balanced between the carriages. Some hung out over the tracks with a ledge for a foothold. The insides of the carriages were black with people. In the middle of one carriage, however, a narrow sliver of light from the window on the opposite side of the train was visible to me as I stood on the platform. The people inside the carriage were willing to help me into the carriage to stand in that remaining space.

Two men leaned out the window and pulled me inside. They placed their hands under my armpits, and they hoisted me inside, over the heads of those who were fortunate enough to have seats.

Above the windows were luggage racks, running in a continuous line about the four walls of the carriage. While the racks were tightly packed with goods, some of the more agile travelers were able to perch on the edge of the racks and make their way up and down the length of the carriage, swinging above our heads. Their feet were bare, and they wore loose, scant clothing, which enabled them to move along the luggage racks carelessly. They were unable to keep still for longer than a few seconds, and they called to each other in loud voices across the carriage, using a language that fitted none of the three I knew. Now and then they helped themselves to something that attracted them, a package of food or a piece of cloth from a basket.

I saw one of these men make a sudden movement. I turned my head and watched him remove a gold ornament from the hair of a passenger. She did not notice. The ornament was fixed to her hair with great elegance. A lock of hair twined about the gold and formed part of the overall design. In order to take the ornament, the man above her first took a knife from his clothing and cut off both the ornament and the lock of hair.

I stood with my right hand beneath the edge of my jacket, without moving, for the rest of that day and throughout the night.

The carriage became dark and turned opaque, long before night had completely fallen outside. As it grew blacker, the passengers quieted down. Those who had spent the journey shifting about in the luggage racks also settled down and remained perched in one spot.

The feet of one of these men hung before my face. I fixed my eyes on his toenails, for in the darkness of the carriage they caught what little light still intruded from outside. Finally, when it had become as dark outside the carriage as within, the toenails disappeared.

At dawn the train arrived. My teacher was standing, watching the gray light, waiting for me. So closely did his clothes and skin match the grays of the platform and the dawn that many of the hurrying passengers, disembarking, bumped into him.

We greeted each other in the high language, and we shook hands. He bowed slightly over our clasped hands while I stood straight and firm.

"Excellent," he murmured. "You are a diligent pupil and have learned your lessons well."

I lowered my eyes before his praise.

It was then that I saw that the front of my jacket was stained with the brown of my blood. With my left hand I touched my ears and found that the lobes, bearing the earrings, had been cut off.

My teacher said: "The last step of the journey you must take alone."

I made my way to the sea. Waiting for me was a small boat. Three crewmen were darting about preparing to sail. When they saw me standing on the quayside, they stopped their work for a moment and helped me on board. They spread a hessian sack on the deck so that I could sit in comfort.

We sailed until we came to a small, round island with a hill in the middle. There I alighted and went to sit on top of the hill. I sat with my back straight, my legs crossed. My hands rested on my knees. I gazed at the ground before me.

I now found that my body was hollow. And inside myself I discovered a small amount of room, a private space, in which to move.

TWELFTH NIGHT, OR THE PASSION

This is the twelfth night that I have sat here in my bed, passionately waiting for Allan to telephone. My yellow foolscap writing pad rests on my knee. I bite the fingernail of my left index finger. My dreadful cat is leaping about, knocking bric-a-brac to the floor before settling down for the night. I read bits of this and bits of that, and think. And I wait.

I have just read in a teacher's guide to literature the depressing information that in the typical comedic plot someone is denied his or her rightful place in society and ultimately overcomes the denial. I have had to put that book down. The idea of Olivia and Viola actually getting what they want is too much for me. The whole idea of comedy makes me want to cry.

Twelve nights ago Allan and I spoke on the telephone. He said he would telephone me as soon as he got back from Ireland. Family business. But he does not seem to return to London, and he does not telephone.

I have had several brilliant thoughts for this term. I will play a recording of a Cole Porter song to demonstrate imagery (idea purloined from American textbook) and I will show my class a picture of Michelangelo's Moses, to foster a discussion of versions of reality and an awareness of word choice (idea from Sigmund Freud).

So far tonight I have received two brief calls. The first was from Louise, who writes novels with a zest I envy. She was returning my call and boning chicken for tomorrow night and could not talk at length. The other was from a student who wanted to transfer to my section and needed to know the assignment for Monday.

The assignment is to write about something that happened, something autobiographical, a memory. The student said he had already perspired over a two-page prose monologue for Section Three, before he found out that Section Three was over-enrolled. I told him there was no need to perspire over the something-that-happened-or-a-memory assignment.

"Oh, it was perspiration of joy," he said. "I love to write."

At the first meeting of my class, three nights ago (the ninth night that Allan did not telephone), I read to my students, to inspire them for the assignment, a little something by Harold Pinter, a man I find very attractive these days:

> I saw him again today. He looked older.
>
> We walked, as we always used to do, along the promenade, up to the pier, along the pier, back down the pier, and back. He was more or less more or less the same, but looked older. I asked him if I had changed. He said no, as far as he could see. I said no, probably I had not. He said he could see no sign of it. If anything I looked younger. I charged him with jesting. He said no he was not. He pointed out that he had used the phrase *if anything*. *If anything,* he said, and turned his eyes, still bright, on me, *if anything* you look younger, *if anything*. If anything you look older, I said. There's no if anything about that he retorted, none whatsoever.

I wrote Allan a love letter last week, and sent it off, to Dublin. I am not accustomed to committing myself on paper like that. I called him the sun, the snow, and the music. Perhaps it fell into the wrong hands. Perhaps he thinks someone else wrote it, in jest.

Every twenty minutes the train to Kew Gardens and Richmond rumbles by, and also every twenty minutes the return train to Broad Street rumbles by. Each train shakes the floor and the bed. The track is two hundred feet away, and I am four stories up in a Victorian mansion, sitting here in my bed, shaking when trains go by. My friend Elspeth, who grew up on this street, often reminds me that these houses still suffer from bomb damage and could fall down at any time. There is one up the hill on Tanza Road which has had to be shored up, all these decades later.

And still Allan does not telephone.

Is Moses clutching, holding, stroking, thrusting his fingers into, or merely touching his flowing beard? I will ask my students. Is he about to spring up, or has he sprung and is now sitting back?

In an old diary I wrote once: "I shall never forget the splendor of the fishing boats of Sibolga at sunset." I have no recollection of the fishing boats or the sunset. But I do remember eating an omelette for breakfast in a Chinese restaurant in Sibolga.

I visited Nottingham recently, for the first time, to see Cecil and Mabel, an old couple who used to live next door. They are fond of me and still think of me as seventeen. They made me afternoon tea and brought out old snaps. They showed me a photograph in which I am wearing a white skirt, a pink-and-white striped blouse with puffed sleeves, and white gloves. I am sitting between them in the lounge of a P & O liner that was about to take them to Sydney. I remember the skirt and blouse, but I have no recollection of going down to see them off or of sitting in that lounge. But I am definitely in the photograph. I must have been there. I was interested to see myself like that and to see that I looked quite pretty at the time.

After visiting Cecil and Mabel I drove north a bit. On the map Sherwood Forest was marked green, to the left, but there was no forest that I could see. Just land, farms. I was hoping to come across a small tribute to Robin and Marian, a statue at a crossroads or something to that effect.

And that wretched man does not telephone. Tomorrow night will be the thirteenth night. If he telephones then, I will not be here. I shall be eating boned chicken with Louise, and there will also be one gynecologist and one jogging businessman present.

The fourteenth night I am going to the opening of an exhibition of photographs of twins—identical twins with intense relationships. I shall go with my friends Barbara the artist and Gary the classics scholar. Gary ordered a black T-shirt with "Professor Schwartz" printed across the chest, and he wore it to his first class this week. He said he was tired of students not remembering his name even after a year. To the exhibition of twins, Barbara and Gary plan to wear identical outfits. They kindly said I could wear the same outfit, if I wanted, and we could go as triplets. I said it would spoil the effect. I can manage on my own. I'll wear my denim skirt, Indian blouse, and sandals as usual. Or else my pink dress.

The fifteenth night I will be cooking lasagna for a potter, a lawyer, and an Israeli spokesman. If Allan telephones me that night, at least I'll be home.

The sixteenth night is my class. The Moses discussion.

I have a friend, not a close friend, the husband of a friend, a man who rarely talks in company. He is a psychiatrist who makes a point of kissing on the cheek men who are in his field. He often asks patients to bring in photographs. He says photographs are very telling. He himself has a photograph from his bar mitzvah, in which he stands between his parents, and he emphasizes with some delight the word *between*. He points out that his mother's hands are clenched, although her face is giving a big smile. His mother still insists that she is not clenching her fists. She is merely holding a small bottle of aspirin out of sight.

The class after the Moses class, that will be the twenty-third night that Allan will not have telephoned. I plan to take my portable record player and play,

You're the top,
you're the Colosseum,
you're the top,
you're the Louvre Museum,
you're a melody
from a symphony
by Strauss.
You're a Bendel bonnet,
a Shakespeare sonnet,
you're Mickey Mouse.

Imagery. I will also read,

O my luve is like a red, red rose,
That's newly sprung in June:
O my luve is like a melodie,
That's sweetly played in tune.

And my luve does not telephone me. We stood on Westminster Bridge early one morning just as the sun was rising, Allan and I. He did not say, "Earth has not anything to show more fair," although he might well have. I think he remarked, speaking of Isabella, that there are people who talk about love and people who love.

The assignment for the following week, the thirtieth night, will be to write a story in simple sentences, no dependent clauses, and then to write a story in questions. Max Frisch writes to himself in questions:

1 .Are you sorry for women?
2 .Why? (Why not?)
3 .When a woman's hands and eyes and lips betray excitement, desire, etc., because you touch them, do you take this personally?

Why do I sit here waiting for twelve nights for a phone call? My mother used to ask, "Why did you leave your plimsolls out in the rain last night?" Must a question be a reproach?

"Whose Life Is It Anyway?" I asked wittily, even flirtatiously, of my luve, one night when we were talking about life.

"Every Good Boy Deserves Favor," he answered.

"You mean Fruit," I said.

He said no, he meant Favor. And of course I gave him mine, happily.

What I am remembering right now is his face, which is often sad, and the twinkle in his green eye, and the crinkle at the corner of that green eye. My luve.

On Waterloo Bridge, he told me a joke that made me laugh and laugh. A traveler comes to the town of Mercy in the Australian outback. He is very thirsty. At the pub he begs for beer. They have only koala tea. That'll do, says the traveler. He takes a mouthful. And he has to spit it out. This tea is full of lumps, he cries. And they reply: What do you expect? The koala tea of Mercy is not strained.

Literature is my luve's field.

What I am remembering now is waking up that first morning suddenly at six and finding him already awake looking at me. That nice face on the pillow, not sad at all, and those green eyes, just looking at me. And I am remembering feeling very happy.

We have also laughed at Woody Allen's Irish poem, in which a man is given to falling down and imitating a pair of scissors.

We walked from Waterloo Bridge along the south bank to *The Passion*. I should have realized then that this was a sign. They had taken all the seats out of the theater. We all had to participate. We stood there and milled about. Suddenly the woman standing next to me started shouting, and the play had begun. And when Pilate asked us who should be set free, I wanted to call out "Jesus." But everyone said "Barabbas," as they ought to, and poor Jesus had to bear that heavy cross round and round that theater. I had never stopped to think before just how it was done. He lies down on the cross, they hammer, and then they hoist him up. I would like to change the ending of that story, and also the endings of *Romeo and Juliet* and *La Traviata*.

There is a man who has written a book called *The Only Two Ways to Write a Story*, and it begins, "There are two, and only two, ways to write a story." This book sits in the stacks next to *How to Write and Make a Million Pounds*. The two types of stories are type (a) in which a man has to achieve something, and type (b) in which a man has to decide something.

All very well, but what about plain obsession?

Two days ago I took an inter-city train to Wolverhampton, one of England's less attractive cities (two hours), then a smaller train to Shrewsbury (one hour), then a smaller train on a single track across Wales to Aberystwyth (two hours), and I stood on the gray pebble beach among the Welsh in their overcoats, looking out over the Irish Sea to see if I could catch a glimpse of my love. Behind me Punch was beating Judy, and I learned at the station that "Allan" is Welsh for "Way Out." I took the trains back to London and sat beside a man who writes BBC news and plays. He shared his supper with me, and we talked the whole way, a thing the English rarely do.

I am going to ask my class to write about an obsession, a passion. I'll tell them Colette's cat story, to illustrate. A man loves his cat. He caresses and pets his cat. He ignores his wife. The cat gloats. It gives the wife smug looks. The man goes out. The cat sits on the window sill. The wife pushes it out. It falls down several stories. The man returns. He cradles the cat in his arms. It now needs more attention than ever. It continues to gloat and give those smug looks.

Enough. It is one a.m. The bed stopped shaking long ago. And Allan has not telephoned. He will not telephone. If anything, I am older and wiser. If anything. And then I discover that my wretched cat is lying on top of my telephone and has nudged the receiver out of its cradle. I'll kill the cat. I chase it around a bit. Then the phone rings.

It is Allan.

Why have I been on the phone all night? What kind of question is that? Can he live with me and be my love? What kind of ending?

RECONSTRUCTION OF AN EVENT

It is a Tuesday morning. The doorbell wakes her up. She may have heard the footsteps on the concrete path leading to the front door just a second or two before the bell rang. The sun is high enough to light up the lime-green umbrellas and lollipop-pink houses printed on her curtains. The jacaranda tree outside her bedroom window casts a shadow on the wall. She has overslept.

Does it matter that it is the shadow of a jacaranda? Rather than dwell on the shadows and the type of tree casting them, just state what time it is. No scene setting, no exposition.

It is a Tuesday morning. The doorbell wakes her up. She has overslept. It is nine o'clock. There is no sound in the house. No footsteps. She guesses that everyone has gone to work and forgotten her. The doorbell rings. She intends to get up and answer it, but instead decides to spend the day, and possibly all days thereafter, in bed sleeping. She closes her eyes and begins the drift back to sleep. The doorbell rings. She sits up with difficulty. Good manners prevail. It is rude not to answer and one spends years learning not to be rude.

It is not plausible, never to have been rude. Also, she has to get up sooner or later, so why not answer the door? Why this repeating of the doorbell rings, the doorbell rings? Also, her thoughts and wishes are irrelevant and throw no light on the matter. It is necessary to state only what happens. No opinions.

The doorbell rings. It is nine o'clock. Tuesday morning. She came in the night before, expecting them to be waiting up for

121

her. All was quiet, and she was grateful. The father normally lies awake whenever she goes out at night. He longs to sleep. Then, after she comes home, he tosses and turns and grunts and growls in bed and finally gets up to walk around the house and let it be known that he has had no sleep and that nothing has gone unnoticed. The next day he gives a speech to the effect that the daughter is giving him gray hairs and driving him to an untimely grave. He often composes his epitaph, beginning ''They will rue the day'' and ending ''and they will all be sorry when I'm gone.'' The whole thing has become a laughing matter, a family joke.

No background. None of the above is necessary or necessarily true. Just what happens.

She goes out, comes home late, and goes to bed. The doorbell rings. It is nine o'clock the next morning. Tuesday. She stands up then she falls right over. She lies on the floor. It feels pleasant enough. She can stay right where she is on the floor and continue sleeping. The doorbell rings again. She crawls to the door, hauling her dressing gown around her. She uses the door jamb to hoist herself up. In the hallway are her mother and her younger brother. They are steadying themselves against the walls. The smell of gas is everywhere. ''Is it an earthquake?'' she inquires. The brother starts laughing, staggering away from the wall, then back again to continue leaning against it. She has never heard him laugh so much. ''In case of earthquake, stay in the doorway. Safest place,'' the brother says, laughing and laughing.

Not credible. They all think that there is an earthquake just because they are a bit dizzy and have to lean against walls? Simply not possible in this part of the world where there are no earthquakes. But if they believe there is an earthquake, why does the brother laugh? An earthquake is serious business. Don't they smell the smell? Don't they immediately know that something is wrong? Do they really stagger and sway like that?

The doorbell rings. The mother, the brother, and the daughter get up to answer it. They arrive in the hallway at the same time. The mother feels her way along the walls to the front door and opens it. .She has an arm through one sleeve of her dressing gown. The other sleeve hangs loose over her shoulder and she clutches it to her heart.

There is no need for her to feel her way along the wall. There is no earthquake. Why does she move so slowly? Is that supposed to be a symbol of something? Why the fancy language, clutching things to hearts? Just the facts. What happens.

The mother rushes to the door and opens it. No doubt she has her dressing gown on properly. No one has said anything at all. It is the piano tuner at the door. He has come to tune the pianola. He has arrived early. "It's an earthquake. Stay where you are," the brother calls. He is laughing.

The piano tuner sniffs. "What's the smell?" he asks. "Not me, I didn't do it. I didn't make no smell," says the brother. The daughter laughs. She thinks she will die of laughter. The mother turns her head slowly, more or less in the direction of her children.

There is no earthquake. No one is dizzy. Also inconsistent. The mother has already rushed to the door. There is no need for slow head turning, if any head turning at all.

The mother says, "Don't speak that way in this house." The brother says, "I didn't do it, that's all I said." The tears roll down his cheeks. The mother groans and leans against the wall. She shakes her head as if she has a drop of water in her ear. "Where's your father?" she whispers. The brother says, "When roses are red they're ready to pluck, when a girl's sixteen she's ready to drive a truck." The mother says, "You ought to be ashamed of yourself."

No earthquake, no dizziness, no laughter, no elaboration, no metaphors. What happens.

The mother opens the door. It is the piano tuner. He has come to tune the pianola. He has arrived early. He says, "What's the smell?" He walks past them into the kitchen. "Everything's turned off in here." He is checking the gas jets on the stove. "What else have you got that's gas that could be leaking?" The mother replies, "Everything in this house is gas. It's cheaper. We get the appliances at a discount. Everything's gas."

The brother says, "Appliances and people, both." The piano tuner says, "What about in the laundry?"

Enough with the reconstructed dialogue. The facts. What happens.

The piano tuner says he can smell gas. The mother runs into the kitchen. She checks the gas jets. She throws open the windows and the back door. The piano tuner stays standing politely at the front door. The mother takes the daughter by the arm and leads her into the back garden. She leans her against the jacaranda tree and goes back to get the brother. The daughter holds on to the gray trunk and looks at the house. She sees the kitchen door painted blue, the window with her curtains, and the laundry door downstairs, also blue.

No trees, no doors, no curtains, no excursions into anyone's head. No fabrications. Only what happens. It does not matter, the tree or the color blue. Forget the build-up and the climax. Just what happens.

The piano tuner stays at the front door. The mother rushes down the back steps to the laundry. The brother and daughter are following more slowly. The mother rushes back to the stairs and calls to the piano tuner to come and help. The daughter is at the top of the stairs and starts to come down. The mother orders her to stay where she is. The daughter walks on down and goes to the laundry door. There are rags and newspapers stuffed into the keyhole and the vents in the door and into the space between the door and the floor. The smell of gas is everywhere. The door is not locked. She pushes it open, coughing and retching at the gas. She holds her nose and goes in and turns off the laundry gas outlet which has been left on by mistake. Then they all go upstairs and wake the father up and they all have breakfast. The piano tuner tunes the pianola.

Not so. That pianola never got tuned.

The daughter stays at the top of the stairs, as she is told.

The smell of gas is everywhere. It is the mother who rushes down and opens the laundry door. All the rags and newspapers fall to the floor. The father lies there on the floor on a spare mattress that is stored in the laundry. His face is next to the outlet. He lies next to the dirty clothes. He looks as if he wants to be found in time. They drag him out into the air, near the jacaranda, and he revives.

No tree, no embellishments, no opinions, no lies.

It is a Tuesday morning. It is nine o'clock. The doorbell wakes them up. The smell of gas is everywhere. They have overslept, drugged by the gas. The mother opens the door. The piano tuner has come, early. The mother rushes to the kitchen. She checks the gas jets. She opens the back door and rushes down to the laundry. The brother and daughter follow her. There are rags and newspapers stuffed into the keyhole and the vents in the door and into the space between the door and the floor. The door is not locked. The mother opens the door. The father lies there. He is dead, having gassed himself. Less than half a minute has passed since the doorbell rang. If the piano tuner had not come early, they would all be dead now.

Later they remember that the daughter was out late and was the last to go to bed. They ask why she did not notice the absence of the family joke and why she did not notice the smell of gas and why she did not avert the tragedy.

No, nobody actually asks anything like that. No need for denouement. This is an ordinary family, one of many such families in houses on streets. Nothing distinguishes it from the others except, today, this event.